GRIP OF DANGER

Before Ruff Justice ever laid eyes on Dawn Sky, he heard that the beautiful Indian girl had been seen astride a racing horse, riding with her proud breasts bared and with the head of a slain white man in her hand.

Then he met her. First face to face. And now body to body.

Dawn Sky clung to him, her breath soft and warm against his throat, her breasts against his chest, her moist lips moving across his shoulder and throat to his mouth.

She made a tantalizing silhouette in the darkness, catlike and lithe. And as her warm hand reached out to grip his manhood, Ruff Justice gave no thought to the dead man's head . . . he was too busy pulsing with life. . . .

Wild Westerns by Warren T. Longtree

(0451)

- [ ] RUFF JUSTICE #1: SUDDEN THUNDER   (110285—$2.50)*
- [ ] RUFF JUSTICE #2: NIGHT OF THE APACHE   (110293—$2.50)*
- [ ] RUFF JUSTICE #3: BLOOD ON THE MOON   (112256—$2.50)*
- [ ] RUFF JUSTICE #4: WIDOW CREEK   (114221—$2.50)*
- [ ] RUFF JUSTICE #5: VALLEY OF GOLDEN TOMBS   (115635—$2.50)*
- [ ] RUFF JUSTICE #6: THE SPIRIT WOMAN WAR   (117832—$2.50)*
- [ ] RUFF JUSTICE #7: DARK ANGEL RIDING   (118820—$2.50)*
- [ ] RUFF JUSTICE #8: THE DEATH OF IRON HORSE   (121449—$2.50)*
- [ ] RUFF JUSTICE #9: WINDWOLF   (122828—$2.50)*
- [ ] RUFF JUSTICE #10: SHOSHONE RUN   (123883—$2.50)*
- [ ] RUFF JUSTICE #11: COMANCHE PEAK   (124901—$2.50)*
- [ ] RUFF JUSTICE #12: PETTICOAT EXPRESS   (127765—$2.50)*
- [ ] RUFF JUSTICE #13: POWER LODE   (128788—$2.50)*
- [ ] RUFF JUSTICE #14: THE STONE WARRIORS   (129733—$2.50)*

*Price is $2.95 in Canada

Buy them at your local bookstore or use this convenient coupon for ordering.

NEW AMERICAN LIBRARY,
P.O. Box 999, Bergenfield, New Jersey 07621

Please send me the books I have checked above. I am enclosing $_____
(please add $1.00 to this order to cover postage and handling). Send check
or money order—no cash or C.O.D.'s. Prices and numbers are subject to change
without notice.

Name _____

Address_____

City_____ State_____ Zip Code_____
Allow 4-6 weeks for delivery.
This offer is subject to withdrawal without notice.

RUFF JUSTICE #15

CHEYENNE MOON

By
Warren T. Longtree

A SIGNET BOOK

NEW AMERICAN LIBRARY

PUBLISHER'S NOTE

NAL BOOKS ARE AVAILABLE AT QUANTITY DISCOUNTS WHEN USED TO PROMOTE PRODUCTS OR SERVICES. FOR INFORMATION PLEASE WRITE TO PREMIUM MARKETING DIVISION, NEW AMERICAN LIBRARY, 1633 BROADWAY, NEW YORK, NEW YORK 10019.

Copyright © 1984 by New American Library

The first chapter of this book appeared in *The Stone Warriors*, the fourteenth volume of this series.

SIGNET TRADEMARK REG. U.S. PAT. OFF. AND FOREIGN COUNTRIES
REGISTERED TRADEMARK—MARCA REGISTRADA
HECHO EN CHICAGO, U.S.A.

SIGNET, SIGNET CLASSIC, MENTOR, PLUME, MERIDIAN AND NAL BOOKS are published by New American Library,
1633 Broadway, New York, New York 10019

First Printing, August, 1984

1 2 3 4 5 6 7 8 9

PRINTED IN THE UNITED STATES OF AMERICA

RUFF JUSTICE

He knew the West better than any man alive—a hostile, savage land rife with both violent outlaws and courageous adventurers. But Ruff Justice had a sixth sense that kept him breathing and saw his enemies dead. A scout for the U.S. Cavalry, he was paid to protect the public, and nobody was faster at sniffing out a killer, a crook, a con man—red or white, at close range or far. Anyone on the wrong side of the law would have to reckon with the menace of Ruff's murderously sharp stag-handled bowie knife, with his Colt pistol, and the Spencer rifle he cradled in his arms.

Ruff Justice, gentleman and frontier philosopher—good men respected him, bad men feared him, and women, good and bad, wanted him with all the wildness of the Old West.

1.

Barton McGinnis hailed the gold camp again, but there was no answer. He didn't like the look of things, didn't like the feeling crawling up his spine.

McGinnis had spent the better part of his adult life on the Dakota plains. He had hunted the big herds and tried his hand at prospecting. He had wintered out along the Heart River when there wasn't a white man within a hundred miles, when the Sioux still were astonished to see a thunder gun, when it was no rare thing to go a year without seeing another man of any kind. Barton McGinnis had married and shed three different Indian wives. He had taken a grizzly bear with nothing but his bowie knife (paid the price of one eye and three fingers for that bit of work), lost most of one ear to frostbite, and been punctured with arrows so many times that he felt close kin to the porcupine.

A man has to have a certain sort of sixth sense to endure that kind of life. Barton McGinnis believed he had it. If he did, it was aching now.

He started walking his gray horse down the long sandy bluff that faced the shallow, rapidly flowing Heart River. The willows shifted in the wind, which blew down from the north. It was a gray and dreary day.

And something was damn sure wrong.

McGinnis held his horse up. He slipped the cover from his repeating rifle and sat staring at the gold camp, unable to make sense out of it.

"Hello the camp!" he tried again, but there was still no answer. The horses grazed off to one side. They had been hobbled and there they still stood, tails turned to the wind. Well—it wasn't Indians then. Not if they still had their horses.

"What in hell?" Barton now noticed the tracks for the first time.

A single unshod pony had crossed the river here. It had, in fact, crossed the river at least a dozen times. Barton looked warily toward the willow brush that fronted the Heart, looked again to the camp, and shook his head, not liking the smell of this at all.

The rider, whoever it was, had crossed and recrossed the river at this point. Always in the same direction, meaning that he was riding in circles.

"What for?" Barton asked the empty day. His horse's ears twitched. "What for does someone ride around in circles? Around an empty camp."

A camp that the week before had held sixteen miners, all hopefully panning the Heart and the Little Heart. Green, most of them were, but they had had Tug Gates with them and Tug knew the land. They hadn't struck much pay dirt yet when Barton had seen them last, and Barton had been inclined to think they wouldn't.

He had shared their fire, wished them well, and headed up into the foothills where Little Jack, the Shoshone, had told him there was a good-sized herd of wild horses. He hadn't had much luck with the horses.

It seemed the prospectors had had even less luck.

Barton McGinnis crossed the Heart River, the water going to his tall gray's belly. He didn't like this, didn't like it a bit. That extra sense of his was raising pure hell.

"Hello the camp!" he tried again.

"You just turn around and get the hell out of here before I blow you from the saddle!" a savage but weak-sounding voice said from the screen of willows.

"Just a minute, friend," McGinnis replied, "what's going on here? Where's everyone? Where's Tug Gates?"

"McGinnis?" There was a moment's uncertain hesitation. "Is that you, McGinnis?"

"Damn right it's me. Who the hell did you think it was," Barton said angrily, for he recognized the voice now despite the strange quality it carried. Tug Gates had gotten almighty shy.

"I didn't know. I couldn't tell . . . come on in, Bart. For God's sake, I'm glad you came back! I'm glad it's you."

Barton's frown deepened and he walked the gray up through the willow brush toward the camp. What in the hell was the matter with Tug? And *where* was everyone else?

Barton knew who was waiting for him, but all the same he approached very slowly, his single eye darting from side to side, endlessly searching. The hoofprints of the other horse were clearly defined in the mud near the river. Circling—endlessly circling. Barton shook his head.

"Tug?" he called out. "Where are you?"

There was no answer. The willows rustled in the wind and the river rambled past. Barton McGinnis's horse shifted its feet and blew.

The sound that reached Barton's ears was scarcely human. Low, moaning, agonized, it lifted above the wind for a moment and then died away again.

"Tug?"

Barton's eyes narrowed. He cocked the Henry repeater he carried and started his gray toward the sound. He found Tug fifty feet on.

"Goddammit," Barton said, his mouth twisting up with revulsion. There wasn't much left of Tug Gates. The prospector lay on his side, wearing a twill coat, out at the elbows, homespun pants, and a white collarless shirt. All of his clothes were smeared with blood.

Barton swung down, looking around cautiously as he moved to Tug Gates, seeing the grooves Tug had carved into the sand getting where he was.

They had broken his legs for him and he had dragged himself a long way to find cover. Barton recognized the leg wounds for what they were—Tug had been trampled by a horse, deliberately trampled. Barton thought of the unknown rider, the circling rider, but he couldn't make anything out of that. He walked to his saddle, got his canteen and bedroll, and tried making Tug comfortable.

Tug Gates was in bad shape, very bad. He would be lucky if he lasted the night. He kept trying to talk, but Barton couldn't make much out of what he was saying.

He propped Tug up and tucked the blanket around him. He was shivering badly but Barton had no inclination to start a fire for any reason whatsoever—not until he understood what had been happening here. Tug's babbling didn't help.

". . . in a circle. You know," he moaned. Then his fingers clutched Barton's wrist with amazing strength. His eyes went wide, looking past Barton, into the distance where his memory was reconstructing the episode.

"Where's everyone else, Tug? Dead, alive? What's happened? Was it the Indians done this?"

"Around in a circle, you know, and then the heads all skinned . . . you know."

Barton said he knew. He didn't. He didn't know a damn thing and talking to Tug wasn't helping much. Barton tried again. "The others, Tug. Fifteen men, Tug. Where in hell are they?"

"Over there." Tug's head rolled toward Barton. His teeth chattered violently now. It took him a time to stammer out the words, "You can see them over there. All in a row."

Tug's hand lifted and Barton McGinnis followed the broken, bloodied finger the dying man raised. He turned and walked through the brush and into the prospecting camp. He saw dead fire rings, two pitched tents, the hobbled horses, eyeing him warily. A lean-to sheltering picks and shovels, a few bedrolls stacked together, others laid out as if someone were preparing to climb in.

No one would be doing that. Barton McGinnis found the missing men. Or part of them.

There were fifteen stakes driven into the ground at intervals, forming a circle thirty feet in circumference. There were lines drawn in the sand like the spokes of a wheel from one stake to another.

On each stake a fleshless skull had been placed.

Barton McGinnis had to turn away. He wasn't sick, but he came damn close. Fifteen men! He went nearer, the skulls staring at him, the wind whistling, chanting in the trees.

McGinnis crouched down and examined a skull. Fresh. The skin peeled off of it. The jaw was missing. A cross had been drawn on the forehead with charcoal.

"Damn it all." Barton stood and looked back toward the river. He didn't believe in spooks and specters, in devils and moaning, creeping things—but this was enough to get the better of anyone.

"What does it mean?" That bothered him. He'd never seen anything like it, and McGinnis had seen some things on the plains and in the hills. He walked a slow circle, seeing that each skull had been positioned the same, facing the center of the wheel. Each had a smudged cross on it Outside of that there was nothing to be learned. There were no corpses, no guns, no signs of battle, nothing.

"Only Tug knows now," McGinnis said. "Only Tug and he's not going to know anything for much longer."

Barton crossed the camp but he found nothing else. Gold-panning equipment lay in the river. In one bedroll he found a sack of dust. And of course there were the hoofprints.

"And what, damn me, does that mean?" McGinnis asked the empty day. Those tracks he had seen across the river ran in a circle around the camp. The distance was something like a hundred and fifty feet out from the center of the camp. It was a while before it hit Barton—

The horse had circled the camp fifteen times.

"Jesus," McGinnis muttered. He walked rather rapidly back to where Tug still lay. "I hope to hell you're gone, Tug. Sorry, old-timer, but I hope you've faded away. Because I want nothing more right now than to get the hell out of here."

McGinnis didn't get that break. Tug was still holding on when the plainsman got back to the shelter of the willows. Barton hunkered down to touch Tug's forehead, to offer him a meaningless smile. Tug looked up at the one-eyed man and tried to say something which didn't come out.

"I won't leave you," McGinnis said, guessing at his meaning. "Whoever it was, they won't get you. I'll set watch."

There wasn't much else to do. McGinnis wasn't going to leave the man—he wasn't made that way—and Tug Gates wasn't fit to travel, smashed up the way he was.

Tug hung on and McGinnis crouched beside him, feeling guilty about wishing Tug would kick off. The gold camp was spooky, oppressive. McGinnis was gripping his rifle a lot tighter than he needed to.

The sun was already low in the western sky, coasting toward the broken, rugged hills beyond the Heart, and McGinnis was getting edgy. He sure as hell didn't want to be out here at night. He wished he had a bottle of whiskey, he wished Tug would cash in his chips, wished Little Jack hadn't spotted those wild horses.

The shadows were long beneath the willows. Lengthening, they crossed and intermingled, turning to pools of darkness. The hills were deep in shadow and an owl hooted somewhere. There was still color in the western sky but there wouldn't be for long.

"I want a drink," Tug Gates said quite distinctly. He lifted his head and peered at McGinnis. "I want a drink of water, Bart."

"Sure."

"I'm sorry about this, Bart."

"Don't think a thing about it." There wasn't much water in the canteen. McGinnis propped up Tug's head and poured. Most of it missed the man's mouth. McGinnis patiently tried again. There wasn't enough water to wet his lips. "Hold on, I'll fill it."

Barton rose and walked to the river. He dipped the canteen in the Heart and crouched, waiting for it to fill. A second later he came leaping to his feet, nearly stumbling in sheer amazement.

The horse! There was a horse splashing across the river, being ridden in a lazy circle around the camp. The rider came on and Barton McGinnis, experienced as he was, stood mesmerized, knowing his rifle was back with Tug, knowing he needed it—now!

Still he couldn't move, couldn't force his mind to accept what the eyes saw.

The horse was across the river now, swinging through the willows, loping toward the camp. McGinnis took off at a dead run, long legs flying, arms windmilling. The canteen floated away downstream.

"It was a woman, was what it was," McGinnis told himself over and over. "A woman. A dark-haired woman. Just a woman."

And she hadn't been wearing a shirt.

She had come riding in a slow circle, mounted on a dark horse, dark hair blowing out behind her. Indian? She must have been, but McGinnis wouldn't have sworn to it. It was like nothing he had ever seen—all of this was unreal and she was just the topper. A woman, a young and nicely built one without anything on above the waist riding lazily around that camp, slowly making the sixteenth loop as if there wasn't a damn thing off about it. . . .

McGinnis burst into the clearing and his stomach went cold with fear. His rifle was gone. Tug Gates was still there—but he didn't have a head.

McGinnis heard the horse crashing through the willows and he started running again, running for the river. He looked behind him and saw her plain as day. Young, beautiful, shirtless, a she-demon with savage eyes, and in her hand was the head of Tug Gates.

McGinnis hit the river at a dead run, ripping off his shirt as the cold current clutched at him, swept him away. A rifle shot echoed across the water, and McGinnis saw the half-naked woman sitting on that dark horse, rifle to her shoulder. She fired again and McGinnis dove under, holding breath as long as possible, holding it until he thought his lungs would burst, until he surfaced gasping, choking, his head spinning, far downstream.

There was only a single rose-colored pennant of cloud high in the sky. The rest of the world was dark, comfortingly dark. The river rambled away and Barton McGinnis rode the current, not looking back, not wanting to see anything of her or of the gold camp. He rode the river away and the night things shrieked their mockery from the wilderness shore.

2.

" 'She lay abed all warm and lazy. . . .' "

"I don't think I like that so much," she said.

"No? I'll move."

"Not that. Don't you dare! Leave it in, damn you."

"What didn't you like?" he said into her hair.

"The part about 'lazy.' Haven't I proven I'm not lazy?"

"That's true," he answered thoughtfully. "I really need the rhyme, though."

"Oh," she said obliquely. "Again. Right there."

" 'She lay abed all warm and . . . um, not very lazy. . . .' " He paused, kissing her bare breast, her lips, her eyes. "That ruins it, you see."

"What. When I touch you?" she panted.

"No. 'Not very lazy.' " He started again.

> She lay abed all warm and lazy,
> Her emerald eyes, her hair all maizey. . . .

"What?" she demanded. "What did you say?"

"Lord, you're a one for breaking the train of thought. That feels good too. How do you do that—work those muscles?"

"Are you trying to divert me?" she asked. She breathed through her mouth as her hands groped for him, found him, and gently cupped him in her palms.

"Divert you? Damn, it *is* getting hard to follow a train of thought."

"Maizey," she reminded him. "What in blazes is that supposed to mean? Highly insulting, I'd say."

"Maizey? Don't bite, please—oh, hell, go ahead. You'll draw blood too. Maizey," he said, returning to the thought, "the color of maize. Corn, that is. Golden sweet corn. That's the color of your hair."

"I thought maize was Indian corn."

"Yes?"

"I've seen that. It's all different colors. Red, yellow, *purple* . . . Oh, God, yes! Again." When she could speak again she went on, "Purple hair, for Christ's sake!"

"This maize is golden. Soft and lustrous."

"Soft corn?"

"Never mind. We need the rhyme."

There was a sudden commotion in the room next door and the lean man with the long dark hair lifted his head to look at the wall of the hotel room. "Inconsiderate."

"Please, a little higher. There . . . God, you're good."

"All poets are good."

     She lay abed all warm and lazy,
     Her emerald eyes, her hair all maizey. . . .

"Again . . ." she said breathily.

"She lay abed, all—' "

"Not *that*. This!"

"Gently, woman. It is joined to this body of mine."

The crash in the room next door was repeated and again the man with the long dark hair lifted his eyes.

"This used to be a place of good repute."

"You haven't forgotten me?" she asked from beneath him, and he smiled.

"Of course not. 'She lay abed all warm and lazy'— what are you sighing about?"

> Her emerald eyes, her hair all maizey.
> Tempts a man, nay, drives him crazy,
> And when I lie I will to lay me
> In a field all lush with Daisies.

Daisy laughed and broke her own rhythm. She kissed his shoulder, nipped at it with her perfect white teeth, and shook her head.

"No?" he asked.

"No."

"It needs a little work, Daisy, that's all. Maybe if you listened again—"

"Maybe if you'd finish one thing at a time," Daisy said, and her legs lifted slowly, her heels touching his hard-muscled buttocks, urging him to follow her gentle rhythm. " 'Lay me' didn't rhyme anyway."

He started to argue the point, but since she was right it was difficult to find a starting place. Besides, Daisy was warm and lazy and her eyes, half closed now, were emerald, and her hair, if not maizey, was soft and golden. She was lithe and warm, with delicately scented flesh over her strong limbs. Her breasts were full and round, delicately tipped with pink rosebuds that demanded constant attention. Her thighs were silky and equally demanding.

He leaned forward and pressed his mouth to hers, feeling her breasts flatten against his chest, her mouth gape open hungrily, her thighs spread still more as her hands found his groin, touched him where he entered her, and held him there.

A rolling spasm began to build deep within her, a trembling that caused her thighs to quiver, her belly to jerk needfully. Her mouth bruised itself against his and her body began to arch and twist, to dance with the tremors that swept over her.

She cried out once and her head rolled from side to

side, her hands clawing at him, holding his buttocks tightly, pulling him down and in, while her pelvis ground against his. She carried him along on a rolling, swaying ride for long, breathy minutes until with another soft cry Daisy reached a second climax and he followed with his own shuddering orgasm.

She was warm and damp with light perspiration. Her hands moved in circles up and down his back. Her kisses worked along his long mustache, crept up his jawline to his ear.

"Now what?" she whispered.

"Give me a minute, woman."

"A minute." Her finger touched the dark scar tissue at his shoulder. "What happened here? You were shot, weren't you? And more than once."

"I was cleaning my gun," he answered.

"What happened here?" she asked, touching the narrow scar on his ribs. "Don't tell me you were cleaning your knife."

The banging against the wall erupted again. Something glassy and breakable hit the floor. A woman screamed and screamed again.

"Damn it all to bloody, flaming hell!"

"What are you doing?"

"Getting up—can't you hear that?"

"Don't . . ." Daisy was frightened. He smiled and kissed her forehead softly, letting his eyes linger on her uncovered breasts. "They'll stop," she said.

They didn't stop. The woman screamed again and there was another crash followed by the muted, deep-throated cursing of a man in a rage.

The tall man slipped from the bed, picked up his dark trousers from the back of a chair, and stepped into them. There was a shoulder holster on the bed as well, and in the oiled leather a Colt New Line .41 revolver.

He picked the pistol up and shoved it into his hip pocket. He turned and winked at Daisy, who was wide-eyed with fear, then he walked toward the door of his Minneapolis hotel room.

There were people up and down the hall peering out of rooms, alarmed at the screaming. Some of them withdrew hastily as the tall man with the long hair and long mustache strode toward the room next door.

The tall man knocked loudly on the door and the woman's voice shrieked an answer.

"Please! Please. Stop him. Oh, dear God!"

The man in the hall shouldered the locked door. On the third try the cheap latch flew off the door in a shower of splintered wood and the tall man stepped into the lighted hotel room.

"Get the hell out of here! Mind your own business, stranger."

The man who spoke was naked. On the floor near a window on the opposite wall was a young, dark-haired woman, apparently part Oriental. She too was naked, her only covering the crossed arms she held up before her breasts. Her eyes were bright with animal fear. Her lips trembled as she tried to speak.

"Please . . ." she managed to say.

"I told you to get your ass out of here, boy," the man bellowed. He was tall, heavy in the shoulders but going to flab. He had dark hair neatly barbered and ordinarily slicked back, although just now it was in disarray. The eyes were unique, yellowish and feral. The gun in his hand was a common Colt Peacemaker.

"Leave her alone," the tall man answered evenly.

"This isn't your concern."

"No. Maybe not."

"If you knew what he wants me to do . . ." the woman cried hysterically. "It hurts, oh, God, it hurts!"

"Get out of here," the tall man said softly. "Grab your dress and go."

"Stay there!" The big man was enraged. "Maybe you didn't hear me, mister. Maybe you didn't see this gun."

"I heard you," he answered. "I saw the gun. Hell of a thing to die for, don't you think? Cool down a little, my friend. No sense forcing the woman—get on out of here," he said again to the girl, who was slowly getting to her feet, slowly moving toward the door.

"If she goes, you die, you bastard."

"Maybe." The tall man smiled and his adversary didn't like that. He stood looking at the lean, sinewy westerner before him, taking in the cool blue eyes, the dark, flowing hair, the battle scars that had chiseled at his hard body. The tall man also had a gun in his hand now, a gun that had appeared from nowhere, and the man with the yellow eyes didn't like that a bit.

"Get!" the tall man yelled, and the Oriental girl rushed past him toward the hallway. She hadn't taken the time to dress. She snatched up a blanket and threw it around herself. Then she was gone, her bare feet padding away down the hotel corridor.

"All right. It's just the two of us now. We each have a gun. You don't want to die over this, do you?"

The yellow eyes blazed. For a long minute the naked man stood staring, the Colt Peacemaker heavy in his hand. Then he shook it off. The anger seemed to ebb, the savagery to sift away.

"No." He shook his head. "It's not worth it. Not here."

"No." The tall man smiled again. "It's just not worth it." When he left the room he backed out, pulling the door shut behind him. There were still a few onlookers in the hall and the tall man bowed to them before walking back to his own room.

"Well?" Daisy asked.

"Well what?"

"What did he try to make her do?"

"Listening at the wall, were you?" The tall man stripped off his trousers again.

"I couldn't hear it all," she complained. "What was it?"

"I don't know. All we can do," he said, "is to try everything until we find it."

"I know," Daisy said as he slipped into the bed and reached for her.

"You know what?" He nuzzled her gently.

"What the torture was."

"Yes?"

"The man was obviously a poet," Daisy said. "He made her listen to poetry before he'd screw her."

"Daisy?"

"Yes, Ruff Justice."

"Please go to hell. Or lie back and participate in the sex act I'm about to have all over you."

"My choice?" she asked.

"Completely."

She lay back and Ruff Justice followed her down, glad that she had made the proper choice.

Daisy was gone in the morning. Justice lay abed staring at the ceiling, listening to the comings and goings of the hotel staff and residents, watching the shadows change, the patch of sunlight on the floor creep out from the wall and cross the room toward the bowlegged bureau opposite.

Then with a sigh he lifted himself and swung his feet to one side of the bed to sit, head hanging, eyes closed. It was time to be going, and he had no desire to go. Was he getting older or had he just enjoyed this time with Daisy too much?

He cared only for the wild country, for the long grass blowing in the wind, the calling of larks on the prairie, tne sudden harsh blizzards from out of a cobalt sky, the springtime mountains rife with wild flowers, the endless ranks of blue pines, the tawny flash of a cougar in the rocks, the waddling menace of a grizzly on the prowl. That was where he belonged and yet he found himself in no hurry to return to the plains, to Fort Abraham Lincoln in Dakota Territory.

"You'll end up like Cody if you don't watch out," Ruff Justice muttered to himself.

He was a friend of Cody's, a good friend. But Bill had tasted comfort and luxury and, for a price, turned out a parody of himself. Well, that was fine if that was what he wanted. Ruff had taken a turn through the East and across Europe with Bill and it had been a grand time, but there was something lacking. The smell of a campfire perhaps. The endless horizons. The knowledge of imminent death. There you are, Ruff thought, maybe that's it. Wanting to be near danger. It can't be normal for an organism to want to risk extermination, to walk the edge to see how many times it can do that before it falls.

Justice shook his head. The thoughts were hard going and he didn't feel like thinking that hard. He got up and padded across the room on bare feet to look in the mirror at Ruffin T. Justice, wilderness man, army scout, rough-country guide, poet, scholar, gunfighter, fool.

Ruff grinned at his reflection, picked up his shaving mug and soap, his brush, and a towel, which he slung over his shoulder.

Lathering up, he shaved without dressing, working his way around his mustache, which drooped to his firm jawline. Satisfied with his shave, he stowed his gear away and brushed his long curling hair, which was to his shoulders now.

It was still there; but one day it was going to make a hell of a fine decoration for some Cheyenne's lance.

Ruff folded his ebony-handled razor and put it away. He tossed the towel onto the bed and began dressing.

It was time to travel again and the dark suit and the ruffled shirt in the closet would have to remain there. He stepped into his buckskin trousers and pulled on a matching shirt. His boots were of elkskin, fringed at the tops. Inside the right boot was a sheath with a narrow, razor-edged skinning knife.

Then the gunbelt. A Colt .44 dangling at a moderate distance from the belt, a bowie with a staghorn handle riding the other side. The hat was a new Stetson, white, with a dark, narrow band.

Ruff packed his bedroll, glancing only from time to time at the bed, only from time to time reminding himself how much of a fool a man can be. Finished with his packing, Justice sat down at the narrow mahogany table to write out the final version of Daisy's poem. She didn't care for it, but she was going to have it anyway.

It's only fair, Ruff thought, for someone to listen to a man's labors.

He insisted on that point rather strongly. On at least one occasion Ruff had held his bored and surly audience at gunpoint while he finished his poetry reading.

"People need their culture."

He finished the poem, blew on the ink, weighted the paper down with two double eagles, picked up the big .56 Spencer repeating rifle in the corner, shouldered his bedroll, and went downstairs. It was time to go home and walk that edge once more.

3.

"Morning, Mr. Justice. Bring back anything with you from Minneapolis?"

"Why, they don't let you carry that stuff around," a second soldier said. "Not onto an army camp, isn't that right, Mr. Justice? Why, you'd have a riot on your hands."

"I can't even figure what you boys are talking about," Justice answered with a grin. The soldiers went off laughing. It was still cool, and steam rose from their mouths as they talked their way across the parade ground of Fort Abraham Lincoln, Dakota Territory.

Ruff stretched his arms over his head and started toward the orderly room. He had only arrived the night before and had no idea what was up, although the rumors had reached all the way to Minneapolis: the Cheyenne were raising bloody hell in Dakota.

There were several civilian mounts at the hitching rail outside of the orderly room when Justice reached it. He gave them a casual reading, recognizing the brand of Amos Saxon the cattle rancher and the roan belonging to Ferris, who supplied the camp sutler with beer. The others he didn't recognize.

Ruff stepped up onto the plankwalk and went in. First Sergeant Mack Pierce sat placidly in the eye of a storm of inquiries and demands. Civilians and soldiers tried to get information, orders, and favors from

Mack at this time every morning. Pierce was bulky, flabby, and wheezing, but pure efficiency inside. As someone had once said, he had the body of a cow and the heart of a lion. He took all the hubbub around him quite placidly, directed the soldiers curtly to the duty corporal, sent one of the civilians—a photographer who wanted to take pictures of the soldiers—packing, told Ferris to deal personally with the sutler, and in another moment the orderly room was empty except for one sick-looking young private sitting in a wooden chair across the room. A death in the family, Ruff guessed.

"Mr. Justice." Pierce shook hands without trying to lift his massive bulk from the chair. "How was your leave, sir."

"Fine and cozy, Mack."

"Yes, I'll bet it was."

"Anything doing?" Ruff asked, perching on a corner of Pierce's desk.

"Anything? Isn't it more like everything! Ray Hardistein got married for a start."

"I know you're making that up," Ruff said.

"Am I now? The hell I am. Corporal Gray says Ray was drunk, Ray says he was sober. But he's married to Polly Scott from the Trail's End."

"Well, maybe it'll work."

"Sure, who knows. You can match Thoroughbreds and it don't work half the time. Those two mustangs, maybe they'll click. We had a serious knifing—that young fellah over there"—Pierce nodded at the kid in the corner—"got himself all loaded up on Indian whiskey and stuck his best friend in the liver with a ten-inch knife. He'll hang or do ten years on the rockpile. He's waiting to see which."

The kid, looking sicker than ever and no more dangerous than a fuzzy pup, looked up dolefully at Ruff.

"Tough," Justice said, reflecting again how poorly liquor and youth mixed.

"Yeah. Emerson's going to lose that leg."

"I thought it was nearly healed up." Lieutenant Emerson had taken an arrow in the thigh, but it hadn't seemed dangerous at the time.

"It came back on him. Blood poisoning, Doc says the gangrene's going to eat him alive if it doesn't come off."

Voices drifted to Ruff's ears from the colonel 's office from time to time. Some kind of meeting was going on, but apparently Justice wasn't needed there or Pierce would have sent him right in.

"War talk?" he asked the first sergeant.

"I'm afraid so. Or rumors of same, you know how that goes. People get jumpy once they're out of sight of the fort. Soon everything that happens is Cheyenne or Sioux."

"It usually *is*," Justice said dryly.

Pierce laughed. "You're right. I don't know what this is right off. The colonel stayed in town last night with that General Landis, the retired regiment man." Ruff nodded. "Yeah, Landis bought the Grand Hotel, you know. Invited the colonel in for drinks and dinner. He'll be back soon." Pierce glanced toward Colonel MacEnroe's office. "I hope," he added.

"All right, did you—?" Ruff's sentence broke off abruptly. The door to the orderly room opened and the four men in it all went as still as mice, their eyes as bright. They tensed and gaped and then realized they were unanimously holding their breath.

She was that beautiful.

Blond, stately, she wore a pearl-gray jacket and skirt and carried a little clutch bag. A small gray and black hat sat jauntily on her head. Her eyes were green, moving. Her lips were the color of a blushing peach, pursed. The dress she had chosen was sedate and proper, but she had a figure that a barrel couldn't have concealed. Long-legged, narrow-waisted, full-breasted. It was a moment before anyone was alert enough to realize she had spoken. And her voice was so nice, soft, and modulated that they still didn't answer, dwelling on the tone of her voice instead.

". . . if the colonel is in. Colonel MacEnroe?" she was asking the kid in the corner.

"Miss, he's just a murderer," the duty corporal said, rising. He was trying to smooth back his red thatch of hair with one hand.

"Sit down, Crane," Mack Pierce said sharply. The corporal did so, his eyes still fixed on the young woman.

Pierce had hoisted himself out of his chair, a rare occurrence between meals. Now he waddled forward to stand beaming in front of the girl. "Colonel MacEnroe is expected momentarily, miss. Please sit down and wait."

Justice, still perched on the corner of the desk, suppressed a smile. Pierce was downright elegant when he wanted to be. His manners and diction were perfect. Pierce shot Justice a warning glance. He didn't care to be ribbed about it right now.

"I'm First Sergeant Pierce."

"I'm very happy to meet you, Sergeant. I'm Norah Gates."

"Gates? Not related to Tug Gates?"

"Yes."

"Oh, no. Well, I'm sorry, miss. Truly sorry."

"Thank you," she said simply.

Ruff was frowning. His eyes looked a question at Pierce: what had happened to Tug Gates? He knew Tug casually, hadn't particularly liked or disliked him. Apparently, he decided, looking at the girl, Tug had qualities you didn't suspect.

Pierce returned to his desk, shrugged at Justice, and started to plant himself in his tortured chair. The door to the colonel's office swung open.

"When the hell's MacEnroe getting here? What kind of army is this we support these days! When I was in the war . . ." The rest of the tirade went past Ruff. He studied the man: bulky, red-faced, wearing a straw-colored mustache. His nose had been flattened for him once. With his temper it was no wonder.

Ruff heard Pierce saying soothingly, "The colonel will be here as soon as his schedule permits, Mr. Stuyvesant. His calendar is very heavy just now, as I told you this morning."

The door closed again without Stuyvestant responding. Ruff had hardly heard it all. He sat looking at the woman, frankly appraising her. Too frankly, he supposed, for Norah Gates turned her head away and sat looking at the floor.

The door to the orderly room opened sharply and three men strode in, all looking severe and unhappy.

Colonel MacEnroe looked older than he had when Ruff had last seen him. There were lines of worry cut around the corners of his mouth, lines that his silver mustache couldn't conceal. He looked at Pierce, who nodded toward the colonel's office.

The second man was no stranger to Ruff Justice either. He and Barton McGinnis had once done some trapping together, and on that occasion they had spent three days keeping a party of warlike Sioux off their backs. Sixteen hours they had lain in a shallow buffalo wallow fighting back two dozen warriors. You became close in a situation like that, although Ruff hadn't spent more than an hour with Barton before or since.

Barton looked older too, worried. There was something lurking at the back of his one good eye. Something that looked a hell of a lot like fear.

I must be reading Bart wrong, Justice thought. A man that had seen as much as McGinnis had, a man who had lived out among the hostiles as long as the old plainsman had, doesn't suddenly develop fear like that.

The third man Justice also knew. Their acquaintance had been a brief one, but Ruff hadn't forgotten.

He was tall, broad in the shoulders, with narrow lips and a square jaw. His hair was dark, slicked back, and oiled. His eyes were cat's-eye yellow. The last time Ruff Justice had seen him he had been beating the pulp out of a Chinese girl who didn't want to perform one of his perversions.

Those yellow eyes, topaz eyes, rested on Ruff Justice, flashed recognition, and moved on, turning to the girl sitting quietly across the room.

"Ruff," Colonel MacEnroe said, offering his hand.

"Sir." Ruff took the hand warmly but eyed the colonel warily. When he was that happy to see Justice, something very bad was up. "How are you doing, Bart," Ruff said to McGinnis, who took his hand with his own. His grip was dry, firm.

"This is Lieutenant Neil Ralston, my new replacement officer," MacEnroe said, and the yellow-eyed man bowed stiffly. No one noticed that Ralston and Ruff never shook hands. There was too much on their minds.

The door to the colonel's office swung open again.

"Well, damn me, I knew I heard you out here, MacEnroe," Stuyvestant said. "Do you know how long we've been waiting to see you?"

"I'm sorry, Stuyvestant."

MacEnroe wasn't real sorry. Stuyvestant was the kind of civilian the colonel couldn't take easily, the kind that believed he owned the entire army and that it had been established just for his benefit.

"Come along in, Ruff," the colonel said, and Justice followed along. Neil Ralston didn't so much as glance at him with those yellow eyes. The lieutenant held the door for the colonel and then went in.

The girl was right behind Ruff. She held her purse in both hands. Her confining skirt caused her to move in rapid, tiny steps.

"Miss," Mack Pierce said, lifting a thick, pencil-clenching hand. "Did the colonel invite you to sit in?"

"Why, no," she said, smiling and continuing on her way. Stunned, Pierce was unable to respond.

Justice, who had heard the exchange, winked at Pierce. "It's all right, Mack. I'll take care of the lady."

"I'll bet you will too," Pierce muttered, turning back to his daily report.

When Justice got inside the room and closed the door behind him, there was so much confusion, what with the returning army personnel and Stuyvestant and his crew, that MacEnroe wouldn't have noticed a line of naked chorus girls let alone one small quiet blonde in the corner.

MacEnroe didn't care for noise. He was an orderly man who enjoyed the orderly world of the army. It was civilians who were the bane of his existence, who brought disorder.

Stuyvestant was talking. "We got to get that freight to Morgan Creek, and it's going! You men are posted out here for one purpose and one only: to protect us from the Indians. All right, we demand that protection."

The colonel was stroking the tip of his silver mustache, a gesture Justice recognized. It was indicative of tension and anger.

The colonel said, "Stuyvestant, you know the situation out there right now. All right, it is my duty to protect our citizens from hostiles. However, I can't protect people who wish to take unusual and dangerous actions. If a man rides into a Cheyenne camp, he can't very well turn around and complain that the army's not protecting him."

"I don't want to ride into any Cheyenne camp, Colonel MacEnroe," Stuyvestant said with growing annoyance. "My friends and I, my business associates here, wish to fulfill our contract to the mining camp at Morgan Creek. There are people there who need these supplies. We need the business. What is it, MacEnroe, have we now got an army that's afraid to fight?"

The colonel didn't like that one at all. For a moment Ruff thought he was going to come to his feet in response. He didn't. He sat, furiously dueling with his mustache, glaring at and through Stuyvestant.

"Perhaps if you would listen to some of what I've had to make my decision on ... Bart? Would you please tell Mr. Stuyvestant what we've got out there now."

Barton McGinnis had been leaning against the wall, arms folded. Now his head jerked up and his single eye searched the room as if he were looking for a way out. "Bad, sir. Pretty damn bad just now." Bart scratched his whiskered chin and shrugged as if that was the end of his speech. Everyone continued to look at the plainsman so he went on. "I seen a party of eighty to a hundred Cheyenne up along the Crook a week ago Saturday. Three days later I rode over the sign of half a hundred more. They was moving in the direction of the Tschida."

"War parties?" someone with Stuyvestant asked.

"Oh, yes. Bet your bottom dollar. No travois, no dogs, no women or kids."

"Did you see any bloodshed?"

Barton McGinnis squinted at his questioner, a kid

with yellow hair and bright blue eyes. "I seen some," he answered laconically.

"Where?" The woman spoke up suddenly and heads swiveled toward her. No one seemed to have known she was there except Justice, who hadn't taken his eyes off her the entire time. "Where was the . . . the bloodshed?"

"At a mining camp on the Heart, near the Little Heart fork, miss."

"Did you . . ." The girl was having a rough time. "See the dead?"

"Yes, miss, I saw them." Barton McGinnis had that funny expression on his face again. Fear? Confusion? Distaste? His gaze met Ruff Justice's.

"Well?" Stuyvestant demanded. "What the hell happened out there?"

"Cheyenne raiding party, I reckon," Barton said, and his eye slid away from Justice.

"Was it nasty, Bart?" The colonel wanted it all out in the open if it would help deter Stuyvestant and his freighters from trying to make that Morgan Creek run.

"I reckon." McGinnis looked at the colonel. "I reckon it was bad. Sixteen men, sir. All of them had been mutilated. They'd had their heads cut off, you see. The skin peeled right off of the skulls like nothing you ever saw. Each one of 'em had a cross in ashes painted on his forehead—some kind of ghost-dancer sign, I reckon."

"And the bodies?"

"There wasn't no bodies. I didn't see a single one. Except for Tug Gates, of course. And then a time later he was disconnected from his too."

The woman's scream was piercing, hysterical. Norah Gates was standing, her hands to her lips, patting at them with an odd little, jittery gesture. She looked at

Ruff Justice with those wide green eyes. Then she simply folded up, hitting the floor hard enough to knock her little gray hat from her yellow hair.

It was gusting outside. Dust drifted across the parade ground as a patrol of cavalry moved out. Barton McGinnis leaned against the side of the building. Justice faced him.

"I didn't know she was Gates's sister, dammit." McGinnis had said that at least fifty times already. "I just didn't know."

"Take it easy, Bart. The doctor said she just knocked herself silly. A small scalp cut."

"I know, but it makes a man feel like a fool. Speaking of which, I can't believe that Stuyvestant forced the colonel to let him go out there. Bad business, Ruff. You and I have seen some Indian trouble, but this here, I don't like the taste of it at all."

"What do you figure? Some kind of ghost-dancer business?" Ruff asked.

"I just don't know," Bart said, looking away.

"I thought you had your ideas. The way it was done at the Heart camp, for instance. That doesn't sound like a war party's work. Mutilation, sure, cutting fingers, gouging eyes, setting fire to men. But I've never heard of anything like this other business."

"Must be some kind of magic stuff." Barton shrugged. He was holding something back and Justice knew it.

"Bart, when the army moves out, I'm going with them. I'm going out on the plains, and if I don't know all there is to know, I'm shaving my chances of survival."

Barton McGinnis looked steadily at Ruff, then glanced around them to the right and left. They were alone outside the surgery where Norah Gates lay resting.

"There was a woman doing it, Ruff."

"A woman?" Ruff half grinned, but Barton was serious, deadly serious.

"You see? That's why I didn't tell anyone in there. That's why I haven't told anyone at all. They'd think I was getting senile or drinking too much or plumb crazy. I tell you, Ruffin, at the Heart camp it was a woman doin' the killing."

"A woman shaman? War leader?"

"I don't know which or whether. All I know is that was what she was."

It wasn't unknown, although it was extremely rare. Ruff was put in mind of Woman Chief, a Gros Ventre who had been adopted by the Crow. Raiding Blackfeet hit the trading party she was with and then invited the Crow in for a parley. No one but Woman Chief had the nerve to go into the enemy camp—neither the Crow nor the white traders with them. Five Blackfeet attacked Woman Chief in full view of the upriver trading post. She killed one with her musket and wounded two Blackfeet with bow and arrows. The other two hightailed it out of there. That was the day she earned her name, Woman Chief.

For the next few years she led Crow war parties against the Blackfeet, on one raid alone taking two scalps and seventy horses. After that she was invited to sit with the war councils. Eventually she "married" four wives to tan her robes and perform her many domestic duties, work unsuited to a warrior.

In the end Woman Chief had been murdered by her own people, the Gros Ventre, after a sentimental visit home. That was twenty-five years back, but Woman Chief was still honored by the Crow. Ruff himself was close to the Crow—in fact he had a wife among them—and he had heard the tales of Woman Chief's bravery many times.

Most people hadn't, and would have just laughed at Bart McGinnis. Ruff had seen too much on the plains to laugh at anything he was told. Barton McGinnis was no greenhorn. Nor was he a liar. Besides, a liar would have been anxious to be heard; Barton was reluctant to tell his tale.

"What was it like, Bart? What happened up there?"

And Barton McGinnis told him.

4.

"That's the way it was," McGinnis swore. "Tug was the only man alive in that camp, but he was stove up. He had been trompled by a horse and his legs were broke, his insides all messed up."

"And she came back for him, alone?"

"She was all alone. I saw the sign of one pony all that time. One pony, Ruffin."

"Riding in a circle? One revolution for each dead man."

"That's the way I saw it," Barton said, shaking his head.

"Then that's the way it was."

"I wasn't going to tell that story inside, Ruff. All of it was like a pipe dream, you know? Especially when I think about the woman. Why, man, she was beautiful! A lonesome man's dream, you know? Riding around in that circle half naked, her hair streaming out behind her . . ." Barton clamped his mouth shut. Justice said he believed him, but why should he? Why should anyone? It made no sense to Barton McGinnis himself. How in the hell had that one woman killed sixteen men? It was impossible and McGinnis knew it. But what he had seen was equally impossible.

"You sure she was an Indian?" Ruff asked suddenly.

"Why, dammit, Ruff, what makes you ask a thing

37

like that?" McGinnis was startled. "I'll tell you something: I wasn't sure, no."

"I wondered. You talked about her hair flowing out behind her. When did you see an Indian woman out and about with her hair loose? I never did."

"Nor have I, and there was something else—I can't put my finger on it, but no, I didn't think she was Indian. Not that she might not have been, but I wasn't *sure,* no. That was something I didn't want to tell anyone, not even you. Because if she wasn't Indian, then what sense does it make to you?"

"None at all," Ruff said with a smile. It didn't make any sense in the world.

"Then you don't believe me, after all."

"Oh, yes, I believe you, Barton. I know you and I know your word's good. I just don't understand it and it worries me. I'm going out there and I don't like to walk into the unknown. I don't suppose you want to ride out with us?"

"I'll tell you the truth, Justice. I spent twenty-one years on these plains, but you couldn't get me within fifty miles of that gold camp for all the money in the Bismarck bank. I promised myself that when I was riding the river down out of there—I'll never go back, not until some plain fool like you has cleaned that up. I got shivers like waking up with a snake in your bedroll won't give you. I'm going to be a town sissy for a good while, soak up some whiskey, and find out if there's a woman in this hole with enough courage to tackle a decrepit old fart like me."

The door to the surgery opened and the doctor stepped out. A captain in the cavalry, Dr. Simms had never spent more than fifteen minutes in the saddle to Ruff's knowledge; but then medical men were at a premium, and the army, all of western society, pampered them to a degree. Simms was a drinking man and a battle surgeon more than a hand-holding family doctor. He'd sew you up and set a broken arm, but you couldn't expect a lot of sympathy.

"What are you two doing here? I told you the girl's all right, didn't I?" Simms had his thumbs in his waistband, a cigar in his teeth. "Justice, I can understand why you're hanging around, but Barton McGinnis, you're much too old for this."

"Aw, doc," McGinnis said, inexplicably embarrassed by the surgeon's needling.

"She'll be up and about then?" Ruff asked.

"She's up and about now," Simms answered peevishly.

"Then she's had more luck then most of your patients, hasn't she?"

"Justice, damn you, I hope you need me soon. I can dig out a bullet without ether too, you know." All the same the doctor was grinning. He touched Ruff on the shoulder and sauntered off—a little unsteadily, Ruff thought.

In another moment Norah Gates appeared. She was as pretty as ever, her hair neatly pinned up but for one errant, silky blond strand. Her face was a little paler, that was all.

That changed too as she saw Ruff and Barton McGinnis and blushed.

"I'm sorry, gentlemen. I made a fool out of myself," she apologized.

"Nothing to apologize for," Ruff answered. "Your body let you down, that's all."

"It's embarrassing. I knew that my brother had been murdered by the Indians, but when I heard someone talk about it . . ." She looked pale again. Ruff took her elbow and steadied her.

"I'm right sorry, miss," Bart McGinnis said. He hung his head. He was kneading his hat with both hands.

"You surely needn't apologize, Mr. McGinnis. I suppose I'm going to have to get used to that sort of talk now that I'm out here. Especially out on the plains, isn't that so?"

Ruff and Bart exchanged a glance. Justice said, "I don't know if it's so or not, Miss Gates, but you can't mean you're thinking of going out on the plains yourself."

"Of course I am," she said, and her chin lifted a little defiantly.

"After what you heard this morning?"

"Yes."

"No." Ruff Justice said it flat out. "You're not going out there. Stuyvestant may have gotten the colonel to lean his way, but damn me if I'll see you go, Miss Gates."

"Oh, I'll go," she said brightly. "If not with the army, then some other way."

"But why?" Barton asked. He looked like he might have been suffering a toothache. It was anguish, pure anguish, to think about this young thing putting herself in danger out there.

"Why? Because my brother's body is out there. You didn't bury him, Mr. McGinnis. At least you didn't say anything about it."

Barton looked shamed. The old plainsman, Ruff decided, was getting damned sensitive. "No, I didn't have time the way I lit out of there," Bart admitted.

"There's that and the gold. You said you saw gold dust in my brother's bedroll."

"Miss, I couldn't say it was your brother's. I couldn't swear it's still there."

"Nevertheless, it was there, and I have a claim to it. I'll tell you men both right now so that you'll understand—that gold is all that lies between me and a life as a drudge, or worse. The house Tug Gates purchased in Fargo and moved my mother and me into is mort-

gaged heavily. There's no way I can make up the pay-
ments by going to work, there's no way I can borrow
more on it. Mother's sick and not able to get around. I
have a woman watching her, but if I can't pay her
when I get back, I won't have her either, and mother
and I will both be out in the street."

"No matter," Barton said, "anything is better than
losing your scalp."

"Not poverty and shame," Norah Gates said, and
her chin lifted even higher. If you couldn't give her a
high score for brains, you had to admire her courage.
But she didn't look like any Woman Chief, and a
woman like her wasn't cut out for the plains. Not just
now when things were hotter than they had been in
years. Something was up out there, with the Cheyenne gathering in the hills to make a big parlay.

"I've enjoyed talking to you gentlemen," Norah said
crisply. "Now, if you will excuse me, though, I must go
and speak to the colonel."

"He's not going to allow it," Ruff said, guessing her
thoughts.

"I'm sure he can be convinced."

"Then," Ruff told Barton as she went chuffing off
down the plankwalk, "she's never tried convincing
Colonel MacEnroe of anything." Ruff had, and had
never found it simple.

"That's it for me, friend," Bart said, sticking out his
gnarled hand for Ruff to shake.

"Not going to go out and play with the Indians,
Bart?"

"No." The old plainsman wasn't smiling. "I'll leave
that to you, Justice. I don't figure my head would
make a good billiard ball. You watch out for that
squaw woman, won't you?"

"I ride light."

"I know you do, Ruffin." His hand rested briefly on

Justice's shoulder. "You take care and let me know, will you, if you get up into the hills and find any mustangs running around loose."

"I'll do that," Ruff promised. He watched Bart walk to his horse, swing up lazily, and head off toward the front gate of Fort Lincoln. "You know, Bart, I could almost envy you this time."

It wasn't easy to like the setup of this one. Stuyvestant was taking six heavy freight wagons and a group of greenhorn miners through to Morgan Creek. The army patrol, led by the yellow-eyed Lieutenant Neil Ralston, Ruff's last choice, was going along to protect the wagon train and simultaneously appraise the situation along the Heart. That meant counting heads. Cheyenne heads. The trouble was the Indians would also be counting heads, their way.

And their way, someone's way, suddenly included skinning your head for you. McGinnis's story was wacky, illogical. The trouble was, Ruff believed it. . . .

The door slammed and Miss Norah Gates came stamping out of the orderly room. She stood gripping her purse tightly, staring out at the parade ground, the muscles at the corner of her jaw working.

"Let me guess," Justice said. "The colonel said no."

"I can't understand this; everyone else is going. Mr. Stuyvestant is taking thirty men! The army is sending an escort. Why am I not allowed to go?"

"There's every chance the caravan won't go anywhere near the Heart River gold camp, Miss Gates," Ruff explained. "It will depend on circumstances—weather and Indian sign, among other things. It may be you would have a long ride for nothing."

"But you may go past the gold camp."

Ruff nodded. She was more stubborn than he would have guessed. "If we do, I promise you I'll bury your brother and bring you whatever gold dust there is in his belongings."

"Can I trust you to do that?" she asked. Her expression said, no, she couldn't. You don't trust people to bring you gold dust.

"You can." Ruff shrugged. "I'm not begging you to. Good day." He touched his hat, turned, and walked into the orderly room.

Lieutenant Ralston was there, filling in some of the necessary papers. Ruff vaguely heard Sergeant Pierce asking him where he was from: Louisville, Kentucky. Special skills? None, Ruff thought, that the lieutenant would care to mention.

It was a damn shame that Lieutenant Emerson, a good one, was going to lose a leg and be mustered out while a slug like Ralston was going to have to replace him. But then Ruff was capable of completely ignoring army officers. He'd proven that on numerous occasions. Ralston could be dealt with the same way.

Sooner or later he would try his specialty again—on a woman in Bismarck—and he would be gone or hung before you could blink.

"Waiting for the colonel, Ruff?" Mack Pierce asked. Ralston's topaz eyes shifted to Justice as well.

"Yeah. Wanted to get the orders straight."

"Your orders will come from me," Ralston said.

Ruff Justice began ignoring the man. "And I had a few suggestions for the colonel."

"I'll let him know you're here."

It happened all at once, unexpectedly. Mack Pierce rose and turned toward the inner door. Ruff Justice was slouched against the wall next to the territorial map. Lieutenant Ralston was at the first sergeant's desk, filling in the necessary papers for a newly assigned officer.

The kid made his move. He had been sitting there

all morning, deathly pale, unmoving, his eyes wide with fear. He had stabbed his best friend in a drunken fight, and now, if he was lucky, the army was going to give him ten years of hard labor. A lot of men didn't come back from that kind of punishment. If he was unlucky, well, they would simply hang him and put a fast end to his misery.

The kid bolted for the door and Ruff saw Ralston grab for his service revolver. Justice stepped in and slapped the officer's pistol away as Ralston tried to put one smack in the kid's back.

The Schofield pistol Ralston carried was knocked upward by Ruff's blow and discharged into the ceiling, filling the room with black powder smoke and plaster.

"Damn you, you interfering . . ."

Ruff was already running to the door, Mack Pierce, calling out something, on his heels.

The kid was onto Ruff Justice's black gelding and riding hell for it for the front gate. Ralston raised his pistol again and Justice took his hand at the wrist, forcing it down. Behind them Colonel MacEnroe appeared, his eyes bleary and red, excited.

"What is it, Mack?"

"Johnny Albright—making a run for it, sir."

"Close the gate. Close the gate!" MacEnroe shouted. No one could have heard him, not at that distance. The colonel grabbed the shoulder of a passing corporal. "That's an escaped prisoner. Run him down, Corporal!"

"Yes, sir." He leaped for the nearest horse, which happened to be Dr. Simms's. The corporal heeled it and it leaped into motion.

The kid, Albright, was already through the gate. The sentries fired their rifles high, warning shots. The corporal was halfway across the parade, flagging his horse with his hat.

"He'll never catch that black," Mack Pierce moaned.

"Get a patrol up, Mack. On the double!"

"Yes, sir." Pierce spun away, calling to Sergeant Campbell, who was in front of the grub hall, hands on hips, staring after the departing riders.

"You bastard, you," Lieutenant Neil Ralston said. Then he made his mistake. He put a hand on Ruff's shoulder and spun him to face him. Ruff's right hand clubbed him down. It was a short, chopping blow that caught Ralston flush and sat him on the seat of his pants in front of the orderly room.

"Justice!" Colonel MacEnroe bellowed. "What the hell is this?"

"Ask him," Justice said. He looked toward the gate, seeing nothing but dust. "That was a damn good horse," he said to no one.

"What is going on here?" MacEnroe asked Ralston as the officer gripped the hitch rail and got slowly to his feet. There was a trickle of blood leaking from the right-hand corner of his mouth.

"I want that man thrown into the stockade. He assaulted me!" Ralston shouted.

"At ease, Lieutenant," MacEnroe said. "You know I can't place a civilian under arrest."

"You're taking his side against one of your officers?" Ralston was roaring.

"I said *at ease*, Lieutenant Ralston. I'm not taking anyone's side; I can't see that there's a side to be taken here. Not until one of you condescends to tell me what in the bloody hell is going on."

MacEnroe was getting mad now, and when the colonel got mad, things began to happen. Ralston eased back a step and took a slow deep breath.

"I was completing the routine paperwork for my transfer to Fort Lincoln when I saw the prisoner in the orderly room try to make his escape. I drew my weapon. Before I could fire my gun or command the prisoner to halt, the civilian scout, Ruffin T. Justice, knocked my arm away. My pistol discharged into the ceiling of the orderly room."

"You don't have to make this so official-sounding, Ralston," the colonel said. His eyes were on Ruff Justice, however, and not on his subordinate. Justice shrugged as Ralston went on.

"Outside I called the civilian an unfortunate name and placed my hand on his shoulder. He then struck me."

MacEnroe heard him out. Then, with disgust in his voice, he said, "Gentlemen. I don't have time to act as a referee for two grown men. You want to fight, go somewhere and do it. I can't see that either one of you acted with any particular wisdom."

"He allowed the prisoner to escape, sir!"

"He kept you from shooting Private Albright, who all in all is nothing more than a scared kid. If I have to see him go off to a labor camp, then that will be that. I won't interfere with a court-martial nor counter army regulations—not for any living man. But the poor bastard didn't deserve to be shot out of hand either. We'll find him, don't worry about that. There aren't many places to go."

"Speak to you, sir?" Ruff asked.

"Ruffin . . ." The colonel shook his head and stalked back inside his office with Ruff at his shoulder. The colonel banged the door shut and poured himself a glass of whiskey, replacing the bottle in his bottom drawer. He threw the whiskey down and sat glaring at Ruff. "Why are you always involved in these things, Justice?"

"Some unique talent, I suppose." Ruff grinned but the colonel wasn't in the mood.

"What do you want, Ruff?"

"Ralston. Are you sure you want him leading this

party west? He's only just arrived. He doesn't know the area."

"That's why you're going along, civilian scout." The colonel fought temptation briefly, lost, and poured himself another drink. "What is it, Ruff? Are you worried about that little flare-up outside? I can understand that. He got excited and wanted to stop a murderer. You recognized the fact that the kid was just that, a frightened kid, and stopped him. Let's none of us worry about that."

"No, sir."

"There's something else?" MacEnroe asked impatiently.

"Where was Lieutenant Ralston posted before?"

"Where?" The colonel frowned. "Fort Abercrombie. He knows the plains, if that's what you're getting at."

"It isn't. Why did he leave Abercrombie?"

"He'd heard about you and wanted to see if it could be true," the colonel said with a sigh. "How the hell do I know, Ruff. I suppose he asked to be transferred to see some new country. Maybe promotions are tight back there. I need an officer, Ruff. I don't ask them why they came to Dakota."

"I was wondering if he wasn't moving away from something, maybe," Ruff suggested.

"Like what? What have you got against Ralston anyway?"

"I just don't think he's a man I can work with easily."

"You what! Why, damn you, Ruff, I thought we were all finished with this foolishness. You'll work with this man or give up guide work altogether. As far as the army is concerned anyway. I've put up with a lot of foolishness from you—I've had you up and desert a unit in the middle of a mission. Because you didn't get along with someone! Dammit, unless you've got something particular to say and something criminally damaging about Lieutenant Ralston, I would like for you to go on out and prepare for the patrol's departure, which will occur at oh-six-hundred."

"Can I ask Mack for a horse, sir?" Ruff asked. He was still smiling and MacEnroe didn't understand that. In fact he never would understand Justice. He could be soft or violent, affable or surly, gregarious or moody. He was also the best damned Indian scout on the plains. Maybe that was the reason MacEnroe tolerated him.

"A horse?"

"I mean to go looking for Private Albright. That was my horse he took."

"Yes, all right. Go ahead," the colonel said impatiently. Ruff nodded and went on out, moving with long, silent strides. The door closed and the colonel leaned back in his chair, looking around his empty office.

He looked at his bottom desk drawer, briefly dueled with temptation again, again lost, and stretched out his hand for that bottle of bonded bourbon.

"Ruff Justice," he said softly. "You'll be the death of me yet."

5.

There was frost on the parade ground when Ruff Justice emerged from the barracks to stand alone beneath the starlit sky. It was cold, very cold. Across the way smoke rose from the kitchen as the cook began preparing the morning meal. It wasn't yet reveille, and although a few men were stirring in the enlisted barracks, the camp was silent and mostly dark.

Ruff Justice walked shivering to the paddock behind the barracks. His black horse waited there, eyes shining.

They had found the horse readily enough. Standing deserted in back of the Grand Hotel. Finding Private Johnny Albright hadn't been so easy.

Soldiers and town marshal's deputies searched the hotel, the nearby stable, the smith's barn on the other side, and then settled in for a long hard look. They combed the town and the willows near the river. Private houses had their cellars and attics searched. The stagecoach was stopped at West Fork and the passengers asked to identify themselves.

They didn't find Albright, and Justice supposed that put him in an awkward position if the army ever decided to really probe this episode.

"No matter, horse," Ruff said, slipping the bridle over the black's muzzle. "What that man wanted to do was pure murder. If they ask me, that's what I'll tell them. There's something rotten about Lieutenant Neil Ralston, something evil. He likes to beat up women and shoot men just to see them die. And that means I'm not going to get on well with him, horse."

The black shifted its feet and blew. Ruff buckled the throat latch, slipped the soft bit into the big black's mouth, and led it into the stable where his saddle rested on a sawhorse at the end of a row of McClellans.

"Why, are you going with us, Mr. Justice?"

Ruff looked up to see Reb Saunders, a drawling, lanky Texan with two stripes stitched onto his faded uniform sleeve.

"If you mean to Morgan Creek, I am," Ruff answered, swinging his saddle up onto the black horse.

"Well, I feel a little better about it then. Rumor is things are tough out there."

"They're tough. Who's the NCO on this trip?"

"Cornwall."

Ruff and Saunders exchanged a grimace and a shrug. Cornwall was big and slow and reliable. He had the imagination of a boiled egg and the fighting instincts of a grizzly bear. He was a warrior, you had to give him that, but he wasn't a whole lot of fun to be with. The men gave him a bad time—behind his back—but they knew he would fight when the time came.

"How about this Lieutenant Ralston, Mr. Justice? Is he anyone to speak of."

"If you speak softly." Ruff kneed the balky black and tightened down his cinches.

"Like that, is it?"

"I'm afraid so. I hope I'm wrong."

"Yeah, I do too. Things are going to be bad enough out Morgan Creek way, aren't they?"

"They're going to be bad enough," Justice agreed. He nodded to Reb Saunders and walked his black out of the barn. Reveille sounded sharp and clear as he came out onto the parade ground. The flag was being raised as the bugler lifted his tune to the starry skies. There was a faint pink blush along the eastern horizon. Ruff Justice waited for the last note to die away and then he swung aboard his black horse and rode out of Fort Lincoln.

There was no need to wait for the army patrol. There was a meeting ground arranged south of the town where Stuyvestant and his cohorts, their party now swollen to eight wagons and thirty-two men, waited for the army.

The boys were in good spirits as Ruff Justice rode up. The wagons were in a loose circle, oxen hitched; the horses were being saddled. Morning was cool and there was frost on the willows along the river. There were a couple of fires going, coffee brewing. Some of the men had broken out the whiskey. It was a fine morning; life was just a picnic.

Ruff Justice sat his black, frowning at what he saw.

"Well, they sent you along too, did they?"

Ruff looked down at the yellow-haired, eager kid he had seen with Stuyvestant in MacEnroe's office. "They sent me along too."

"Going to show us how to get to Morgan Creek?" The kid laughed. He was a little cocky, playing up to some of his friends who were lounging nearby, propped up against a heavily laden freight wagon.

"Something like that," Ruff said. His eyes didn't reflect any humor. There was nothing funny going on. These people were taking a group of slow-rolling wagons into the heart of Indian country. They had the army with them and were suffering from some serious overconfidence just now. The whiskey wouldn't help, but something like that didn't worry Ruff as much as the attitude he saw displayed.

Maybe Barton McGinnis should have been brought over to tell his story one more time.

Ruff swung down and walked his horse to the river, letting it drink as the rising sun gilded the slowly rolling Missouri and the trees along the banks came alive with songbirds.

When he got back to the wagons, there was a surprise waiting for him.

"How are you, Mr. Justice," she said. "I thought we might meet again."

Ruff felt his jaw muscles twitch as his teeth clamped together. It was Norah Gates wearing a white blouse, buckskin riding skirt, and a flat Spanish hat.

"What are you doing here, Miss Gates?"

"I'm going along," she said pertly. "Isn't it obvious?"

"I thought the colonel made it clear that you weren't going."

"He made his point clear, yes," Norah said, and her cheeks began to flush a little. "But . . ."

"What's going on here?" The voice was Stuyvestant's. In a buffalo coat and twill pants he looked even broader—less a merchant, more a workingman. He looked Ruff Justice up and down and repeated his question. "What is this?"

"Nothing to do with you, Stuyvestant."

"No? This is my wagon train. It's my concern if it has to do with anything or anyone with it. You stick with the army and stay out of my camp if you don't like it."

"What are you doing, putting it on for the lady?" Ruff asked. His voice was mild, but his eyes twinkled with a message for Stuyvestant. Ruff didn't like being pushed. Stuyvestant didn't answer, so Ruff went on. "I asked the lady what she was doing here. Maybe you want to tell me."

"Sure, I'll tell you. She asked me if she could go along and I said yes."

"MacEnroe told her no."

"MacEnroe don't boss me and he don't boss this train. So what if the colonel told her that? She's got the right to travel wherever she wants and she wants to travel west with the train."

"Yeah, what was the price?" Ruff asked, and Stuyvestant's face went briefly slack.

"That's none of your concern either, is it, scout?"

They were leaning nearer to each other now, getting a little hotter under the collar. The sounds of approaching horses interrupted the discussion.

The cavalry contingent, fifteen men, was arriving. At their head was Lieutenant Neil Ralston, his hat on square, his back rigid as he sat his army bay horse. Beside him was Sergeant Walter Cornwall, blank and stolid looking.

Ralston turned his men over to Cornwall and rode up to where Ruff stood with Stuyvestant and the girl. "Everything in order?"

"Everything's in order if you'll get your damned scout out of here."

Ralston's eyes shifted to Ruff. "What's the trouble here, Stuyvestant?"

"The trouble is the man insists on interfering where it's not his concern."

"Mister Stuyvestant," Norah said, "has kindly allowed me to buy passage to Morgan Creek."

Ralston's yellow eyes danced a little. Maybe it was only the sun reflecting off the river.

"Well, there's nothing the army can do about that, is there? Personally, I will find it a pleasure to have Miss Gates with us." He smiled and gave Norah a little bow.

"Well, then," Norah said, turning to Ruff, "it would seem that you are outvoted."

"Maybe if you don't like the way things hang, Justice," Stuyvestant crowed, "you ought to just stay behind here in Bismarck."

No. No, he wouldn't do that. But just then he was regretting the fact that he had ever left Minneapolis and Daisy Kilbride. He swung aboard the black and rode out at a walk. No one had told him their plans, no one had asked for any advice. Reb Saunders was leading three horses back from the river. He squinted up at Justice.

"Howdy, Mr. Justice. How's things?"

"All right, Reb," Ruff told the corporal. "Looks like it's going to be a long ride."

"Don't it?" 'Reb said dryly. He looked around him and then spat. "It don't shape well from my end, which is to say the bottom of the deck."

"It doesn't shape well from here either," Ruff said. "But we haven't got a lot of choice, have we?"

"No, sir." Reb laughed. "The army damn seldom asks me for my valuable opinion."

Ruff grinned and lifted a hand in farewell. The army damn seldom asked Ruff Justice his opinion either, but if they had, he would have told them that this was the next best thing to suicide and the only good way to handle it was for the army patrol to pull off, taking Norah Gates with them. But like Reb Saunders said—no one asked.

The wagons rolled out an hour later. The sun was warm on Ruff's back. The grass slowly shed its frost and sprang up green and long to be shuffled by the breeze out of the north.

Ruff rode out from the wagon train proper, his eyes on the far horizons, where the Cheyenne roamed. The Cheyenne and the hunting woman, the woman who killed. Justice was inclined to disregard that story, but he couldn't completely. There had been something terrible in Barton McGinnis's expression, something fearful and awed. A child who has seen something evil has eyes like that. No, Bart was quite sincere in his telling of the gold-camp massacre. If he had not been suffering from some sort of delusion, then she was there. She—the woman who came to do evil.

It wasn't a pleasant thought and it rode with Justice as they crossed the long plains, angling slightly north by east. Stuyvestant was planning on picking up and following the Heart apparently. And why not? There was supposed to be gold there. Dead men's gold belonged to anyone.

"And that," Justice said to the black horse, "is how Miss Norah Gates has purchased her passage." If there was dust in Gates's roll, it would be shared with Stuyvestant. Ruff felt sorry for the girl. A brother she and her mother had relied upon dead. The mother sick, and a mortgage on the house. He could understand her determination to come out here, but dammit, it didn't make the move any wiser.

He was still thinking on that when he came across the pony tracks.

One unshod horse moving southward from the Heart. A small horse carrying little weight. Ruff pulled up and sat looking south and then north again. The wind shifted the long grass, and larks called to each other across the prairie. Outside of that there was nothing.

"A lone Indian."

And it meant nothing. Nothing at all. A straggler hurrying to catch up with his band. Why then did Ruff feel uneasy?

No one else did. At dusk they were twenty miles out, a stone's throw from Bismarck and the fort. It was a regular party. Bonfires, plenty of food, good whiskey. There was a man with a squeeze-box sitting on the tailgate of a wagon when Justice rode in.

The army camp he had passed on the way was quieter but no more worried apparently. Justice hadn't seen a single sentry out.

Lieutenant Ralston was eating supper with the wagon train, and it seemed a fair enough idea. Justice swung down behind the chuck wagon, which wasn't much different from a cattle drive's bean buggy, with its many compartments for salt and beans, rice and flour, with a downfolding tailgate for the cook to work off of.

"What's it tonight?" Ruff asked.

"Are you the particular type?" the cook growled. He spooned something onto Ruff's plate from the huge pot on the ground near the tailgate.

"No, I just like to identify it, that's all," Justice said. The cook didn't like it, but someone else chuckled. Justice took his tin plate and walked away toward the fire inside the circled wagons. The men sat in groups of four or five, talking loudly. Some of them were curled up under the heavily laden, high-wheeled wagons already, trying to sleep amid the tumult.

Stuyvestant, Neil Ralston, Norah Gates, and the blond kid, who someone had said was Stuyvestant's son, all sat together drinking coffee. Norah had a shawl around her shoulders. She held her tin cup with both hands and stared into the fire. Her thoughts, wherever they were, were far away.

Ralston's weren't. They were on Norah Gates.

The officer sat there, perched on the crate they had taken from one of the wagons, staring at Norah with those yellow, fire-bright eyes. She was aware of it, because from time to time she would look up and then let her gaze shuttle quickly away. There was no telling what she thought of the attention.

Ruff ate leaning against the wagon. The stew—that

was what it was, what everything was called—was
passable, but there was too much salt and too much
tomato sauce. He was just finishing up when the blond
kid walked up to him.

"Evenin'," Justice said.

"Evenin', hell. Where's my gun?" he nearly shouted.

"Where's your gun?" Ruff shook his head. "Kid, I
got no idea in the world what you're talking about."

The old man was coming now and with him Ralston,
summoned by the kid's loud talk.

"What's going on here?" Stuyvestant demanded.

Ruff shrugged. "I've no idea."

"Why, damn you, look there." The kid was getting
downright annoying, but then Justice had the idea he
was trying to be. "That gunbelt hanging on that peg
had a pistol in it when I went to have my dinner."

Ruff glanced at the peg on the side of the wagon, a
peg used for hanging harness. There was a nice oiled
holster there, all right. It had silver studs pressed into
it. There was no gun.

"Sorry, kid, I didn't see a gun. I don't know a thing
about it."

"Not your good gun, Rudy?" Stuyvestant put in,
shoving his kid aside to get nearer to the empty holster.

"That's right," Rudy Stuyvestant said, nearly shriek-
ing it out.

"It was a special gun, was it?" Lieutenant Ralston
asked. The yellow eyes were alive with amusement.

"That's right, Ralston. It has silverwork on the frame,
pearl handles." Old man Stuyvestant finally decided
that staring at an empty holster wasn't getting him
anywhere and he took up staring at Ruff instead.

"I hung it on that peg so I could watch it while I ate.
And I did keep my eyes on it. I swear to you not a man
walked near this wagon the whole time we ate . . .
except Justice."

"I didn't take your gun," Justice said quietly. "I've *got* a gun."

"He had to have taken it, Pa!"

"I just told you I didn't. My word's generally considered enough."

"It ain't enough for me!" the kid said excitedly. "By God, if you haven't got it, you'll stand for a search."

"You're not going to search me, kid." Ruff shook his head, looking briefly down at the ground and then back up sharply at Rudy Stuyvestant. "Not hardly."

"If you don't have it, Justice," Neil Ralston said, "and I'm sure you don't—why not submit to a search."

"No," Ruff said, "I don't have it. I'm sorry the kid's gun got taken, but none of you is going to put a hand on me to search me. If you try it, you won't much like the result, I'll promise you that."

With that Ruff picked up his tin plate and turned to walk away. The big hand fell on his shoulder and spun him back and Rudy Stuyvestant opened the ball.

6.

The kid was big and he had some muscle in those shoulders. When he hit, it hurt. But Ruff had been expecting it, and when the hand settled on his shoulder and he felt himself being turned, he started ducking down and away from the right-hand shot that had to be coming.

It caught him on the temple, sending his hat flying, but it didn't do a lot of damage. The kid was in a red-faced rage. He bored in on Ruff Justice with both fists swinging windmill punches.

Ruff backed away, stabbing lefts into the kid's face. He heard a cheer go up, saw several of Stuyvestant's men running toward the action. He blocked one of the kid's punches, took one on the jaw, and staggered back, coming up hard against the wagon as Rudy, overconfident now, sensing a quick victory, came in.

Something flashed in Neil Ralston's eyes, something gleeful, and Justice's alert senses picked it up. From his blind side old man Stuyvestant was moving in, a club raised. Ruff kicked out sideways, taking him in the groin. Stuyvestant folded up with a grunt as Justice took another smashing hook to the jaw from Rudy Stuyvestant.

Ralston was standing back enjoying it all. A crowd had gathered now and they were cheering Rudy on. He was doing his best to please them.

Rudy tagged Ruff with yet another right. It drove right past his defense and snapped his head around, driving it back against the wagon. The kid plodded in, working methodically.

Justice had to get off the wagon and he knew it. He took a low left-hand shot to the body and then came up inside with both his fists. The blow caught Rudy's chin and slammed his head back. Blood began to flow from the kid's mouth.

Justice backed away slowly now, jabbing, moving, trying to clear his head. There were nests of birds up there just now and hives of humming insects. He felt someone behind him, felt hands shove him back toward the center of the circle the spectators had formed.

"Kill him, Rudy," someone shouted helpfully, and Rudy came in again, determined to do his best.

Ruff Justice was tired of this, tired of Ralston, tired of the kid and his father, tired of this assignment, tired of catching blows to the head and body. His tiredness translated itself into anger.

He kicked out hard, trying to catch the kid's kneecap. The blow was low, landing painfully, but not damagingly, on the shin. Rudy tried to counter with a right hook, but he had thrown that one enough so that Ruff had the timing down. Justice blocked it, stepped inside, and uppercut to the kid's liver.

Rudy grunted and backed away and Justice followed him, stabbing three straight lefts to the kid's face, which was starting to look just a little battered now, just a little bewildered. He had hit the scout with his best punches and the man was still on his feet—more, he was catching his second wind and his punches were sharp and accurate as Rudy's strength began to flag.

"Bear-hug him, Rudy," someone called. Anxious for any suggestion, the kid tried that. Stepping forward, he took two sharp blows to the right ear but managed to get his arms around the taller, leaner Ruff Justice and hoist him from the ground, trying to squeeze the air from his lungs, to snap his spine.

Ruff Justice slammed the side of his fist down against Rudy's nose, and bone broke. Blood spattered Ruff and the kid, but still Rudy Stuyvestant held his crushing grip.

But not for long. Justice reached out and dug his thumbs into the hollows below the kid's ears and he screamed in agony, his arms falling away from Justice as he stepped back, his face a mask of blood, his shirt torn, mouth gaping open as he tried to breathe through a broken nose.

Justice finished it. He followed the kid back, jabbing, ducking, feinting. He started a right and held it back, crossed with a left, and saw Rudy's knees buckle as the blow landed flush. Somehow the kid stayed on his feet until Justice saw the opening the tired defending arms left, and the one punch he had been saving got through, a short stiff right with all of the weight and balance of Ruff's shoulders and hips behind it. It landed solidly and the kid went down to stay.

Ruff Justice backed away. His dark hair hung in his face. He was smeared with Rudy's blood. There was a small cut and a large lump over his left eye.

Old man Stuyvestant had a scattergun.

"Damn you, you son of a bitch. You might have whipped my boy, but you'll not win this war. You'll stand and be searched, do you hear me, Ruff Justice!"

"Shoot me then and search the body, damn you," Justice said hoarsely. Stuyvestant was going to do nothing of the kind, not with dozens of men standing around waiting to catch a stray buckshot pellet.

Ruff turned on his heel and started away. "Thanks

for supper," he said. He shouldered on through the gathered men and started toward his horse.

Norah Gates stood watching him, and for a moment Ruff thought she was going to call out, to come after him, but she didn't. It was just as well; he wanted to be alone just then, away from men and women and their games.

He straddled the black and rode toward the Heart, dark and coldly gleaming. There were thousands of frogs chorusing in the cattails and reeds along the banks. Justice got down and walked to the river's edge, rinsing his burning face with the cool water. A horse galloped up and the girl swung down.

"Are you all right?" she asked. At the sound of Norah's voice, Ruff rose and turned.

"Sure."

"You broke Rudy's nose, you know."

"Good. I thought so."

"How can you say 'good'? don't you have any feelings?" Norah came nearer, hands behind her back. There was a little edge to her voice. Maybe she had suffered enough from violence not to want any part of it, necessary or not.

Ruff wiped back his long dark hair and planted his hat. "He wanted to break my nose—or worse. It was a contest, you see, that's what fighting is. A contest to see who gets to live or go around without a broken nose."

"But you could have avoided it all! All you had to do was let them search you . . . unless you did take the gun, and you didn't do that, did you?"

"No, Miss Gates, I didn't take the gun." Ruff's head ached dully. He wasn't up to this conversation. "I don't suppose I can explain it to you. It's a gut thing. People just don't lay hands on me, not after I've given them my word."

"It means something, your word?"

"It better. It has to out here. I've promised people I'd come back for them when the Sioux had us pinned, promised that I'd deliver their gold. If my promise is no good, then I'm not worth much."

"Will you promise me something?"

"What?"

"That you'll see I get my share of my brother's gold." She came nearer, and her eyes were starlit, moving. Her hand rested on Ruff's chest. "That no matter what, you'll see that I get whatever gold dust was left in the camp."

"I thought Stuyvestant promised you that," Ruff said.

"Can I trust him?"

"Probably not," Ruff said candidly.

"But you . . ." She was even nearer now, her breasts inches from his chest, her head tilted back as she looked up at him, those eyes shining. Eyes that promised and pleaded and perhaps told little lies.

"I'll do everything I can to see that you get your gold so long as it doesn't risk anyone else's life."

"Swear it." She hissed through her teeth and Justice frowned in the darkness. Norah Gates was beautiful and young, but there was also something too intense about her, something nearly manic. At least there was just now. Her hand clutched at his buckskin shirt, her eyes glowed. Her lips were parted slightly, her teeth showing white behind them. "Swear it!"

"I told you what I would do," Ruff said, and he would never have believed it, but he opened her fingers, pried them open, and moved away from her as she watched.

"I know you will," she said, and then she was near him again, going on tiptoes to kiss him, her mouth hungry and sweet and damp. Her kiss was almost fierce, and then she stepped back, lifted her shawl up over her head, and turned to walk swiftly to her horse, leaving Ruff bemused and unsettled.

"What," he asked the night, "was that about?" Was the woman deathly afraid of something or was she someone to be feared? Was she desperate to have Justice on her side because she feared Stuyvestant crossing her, or was there some other reason? Maybe there was another reason for her being here at all.

Justice walked the black away from the wagons, away from the cavalry camp. He wanted to be alone out there, alone where he could hear and feel the movement of men and spirits around him. The black gelding was a better sentry than any man could be. Ruff himself slept lightly; he hadn't yet awakened to find himself dead—but that was because he didn't take chances.

He spread his roll atop a low knoll where the short buffalo grass grew in brown bunches. The stars were an incredible sight, near enough to touch, bright enough to outshine a winter sun. There was a pale glow near the horizon where the rising moon touched the sky with promise.

With the black hobbled a few yards away Ruff lay down to sleep, but it wasn't going to come easy on that night. There was too much going on that he didn't understand.

Norah. What did she want besides the gold? Rudy. Had there ever even been a gun? Did he really think Justice had taken it or was that some sort of game? If there was a gun and Justice hadn't taken it, then who had? What was the point in it? Could a silver-mounted, pearl-handled Colt be hidden until they reached Morgan Creek?

If we reach Morgan Creek, Ruff thought. He had no

faith in Ralston's leadership, no belief that the officer would take advice if it came to serious trouble.

"And who in the hell was riding that lone pony?" he asked the stars. Who, indeed. A naked woman with a bloody battle-ax or a wandering Cheyenne looking for his people? I'm as crazy as Barton McGinnis tonight, he thought, and it was a night for madness with the confusion of the day, the vast and trackless sky overhead, the long, dark, empty plains below, and away off a coyote howling at the coming moon.

Justice knew even if the rest of the men in the two camps did not. He knew.

The coyote he had heard moved on two feet.

The Cheyenne moon was pale against the dawn sky. There was color along the eastern horizon, like battle fire in the sky, as the sun stretched flaming arms and drew itself above the dark line of the plains.

Justice rose and saddled his black, rolling his bed up tightly, smelling the coffee from the pots boiling a quarter of a mile away. It was a good morning. No one had died in the night.

"Morning, Mr. Justice."

"Howdy, Reb. Any coffee left."

"All you want. Heard you got into a scrape last night."

"Not much of one." Ruff hunkered down next to the campfire and poured himself a cup of coffee from the granite pot. Reb was watching him expectantly, hoping to hear the story of the scuffle with Rudy Stuyvestant, but Justice didn't feel like reliving the moment of glory.

"Good morning, Justice."

Reb Saunders got to his feet as Ralston approached the fire. Ruff just lifted his eyes.

"What is it, Lieutenant?"

"I want you to go out ahead this morning. As much

as five miles ahead of the wagon train. I've decided to stick to the Heart riverbottom. It will assure us of water for the horses and oxen."

"And assure we go through the gold camp."

"That is of no importance whatever to me," Ralston said stiffly.

"Of course not," Justice answered.

"May I assume," Ralston said, growing even more formal, "that you have heard and understand the order? That you intend to comply with it?"

"Yes, Lieutenant," Ruff answered. It was what he had intended to do anyway.

"Very well." Ralston spun on a heel, paused and gave Justice one last scathing glance, and walked away. Reb Saunders was grinning from ear to ear.

"When I grow up," the corporal said, "I want to be a civilian too." Then he chuckled. "You do a man's heart good, Mr. Justice, you truly do."

"What do you make of him, seriously, Reb?"

"Make of that? I can't make him out at all, to tell you the truth." Reb poked at the dying embers with a fire-blackened stick. "There's just some people you get a feeling about, you know? Some you know you couldn't trust when push came to shove, some you wouldn't 'low behind you with a pig sticker." The Texan lifted his chin toward the departing officer. "He's one of them, Mr. Justice. In my book at least."

"In mine as well," Ruff said.

"Mr. Justice," a private soldier called. "When you going to come around the campfire and do some of those songs for us!"

"Maybe tonight. Soon," Ruff said.

"Do that 'Heavy-hipted Woman' one, will you?"

"Sure, Scotty. That's the one we'll do first."

The soldier left and after a moment Reb stretched

and went off too. Ruff sat alone, staring down at the cold ashes of the morning fire, wondering.

Half an hour later he was riding free and fancy across the plains, the horse's hooves marking crescents against the frosted grass. The sun was warm and fiery, making jewels of the dewdrops.

And the lone pony was still out there.

Justice saw the tracks almost immediately.

The unshod pony, the same one, had crossed the Heart in the night, drifted out half a mile or so from the camp, and been halted. Justice knew this because he was now following the tracks of the pony, following it with a prickly sensation working up and down his spine, wondering if there weren't eyes on that knoll ahead watching him.

Ruff glanced back toward the wagons, wondering what Lieutenant Ralston was thinking—if he was watching his scout at all. This wasn't exactly what his orders had been. He was actually circling back now, away from and south of the wagons. Most of the officers at Lincoln would have understood that Justice had come upon something of interest, known that he would report when he could if it was anything they needed to know.

Ralston wasn't most of the officers at Lincoln.

"Hold up there now," Ruff said, and the black slowed and shambled to a stop, blowing loudly through its nostrils. The Indian pony had stopped again. This time the rider had slid down.

"There you go," Ruff said to himself. He got down although he could see the tracks perfectly well from horseback. There was a little clear patch of ground and it had been damp the last few mornings. The dewy earth had taken clear, shallow imprints.

"Little fellow—nope, a damned squaw sure as hell." Ruff squatted down over the tracks, running a finger across one of the imprints, shaking his head. "I don't like this, horse."

He could think of several reasons for a Cheyenne squaw to go ariding. A wild young one might be looking for her man. Maybe it was necessary to send a message to the war party from the home camp and the girl was the only one around to go.

Ruff didn't think it was anything like that.

"This woman's dogging us now. She rides to that knoll yonder and sits watching the night camp. She decides she can't see well enough—or the sun's coming up and she's exposed, so she moves in nearer. This time she swings down. But she's watching. She definitely is watching."

Ruff looked around a little more, found nothing, then he got back up on his black. He could have followed the woman farther, but there was no point in it. She would be back.

To the south, where she was heading, the land was broken up by deep, sudden coulees. Once she got in there Ruff doubted he could keep up. The tracking would just be too tough.

Ruff lifted his eyes, seeing the silver Heart River ramble on away, seeing the tiny dark shapes of the wagons and plodding oxen, the outriders—and there were numbers of outriders, over forty men all told.

"And there was sixteen at the gold camp. It only took one little squaw to do them all in."

He started the black after the wagon train. Today with any luck they would reach the gold camp. That was an unsettling thought, though Ruff couldn't have said why. He would have preferred to veer far away from the camp, although a strange desire to see the slaughter, to discover with his own eyes the truth or falseness of Barton McGinnis's wild story, called him.

There was no putting things off any longer as far as

Ralston and the story of the lone riding woman went. Barton might have been embarrassed. Ruff couldn't be. He had a job to do, and it required him to apprise the army of all intelligence information.

Ralston wasn't going to like the story. He was going to mock it, ridicule Justice. Nevertheless, the tracks were there, the woman existed. The officer would be told; what he did with the information was his own business.

Ruff was riding parallel to the wagon train. Parallel and to the south. The land was utterly flat to the north, but once across the Heart there were scattered trees, mostly oak and cottonwood, a few low knolls rising toward the distant foothills, and a growing network of coulees—all of which made the northern route more desirable with an enemy in the field.

But Ralston and/or Stuyvestant had decided it was necessary to stay along the Heart and pass through the gold camp. It wasn't hard to figure out why. Ruff only wondered what would happen if they did come up with a quantity of gold. Enough gold to make adversaries of them all.

He saw the darting dark figure only out of the corner of his eye. His heart lifted in his chest and he unsheathed his Spencer, starting the black that way with pressure from his right knee as he cocked the big .56 repeater.

Indian, was it? The squaw?

It had to be an Indian, didn't it? He had lost him now, dammit, but he hadn't been mistaken—not about something like that. You lived by seeing your enemies before they saw you. There was no mistake.

A quick darting shadowy figure running south, down that rocky shallow gorge and then—well, he had to be there still, didn't he? Ruff slowed the black and began to circle wide.

The land was depressed here and he could no longer see the wagon train, no longer see the Heart although he could smell it.

Ruff halted his horse. The animal seemed to sense something, to understand that its master was coiled, ready to defend or attack. The black horse stood braced, only its silky dark hide rippling.

Ruff slowly scanned the hillside, looking into the shadows where the rocks bunched together, letting his eyes sweep the sage-covered slope opposite.

He saw him. And when he saw him he knew he had trouble. The enemy was desperate and desperation leads to a sort of mad strength.

Ruff was looking at madness.

7.

Ruff slipped from the black and stood, his back to his horse, peering into the sun as he measured distances and angles. He took his first running step and the bullet from the brush sang past as, racing toward the stack of boulders below and to his right, he hurled himself through the air.

He landed roughly, grunted a curse, and huddled against the rocks as a second and third bullet were wildly fired, ricocheting off the boulders.

Justice had his Spencer and he was reasonably sure he could have turned around, wriggled up to the notch in the rocks above him, and plugged the ambusher.

It wasn't the way he wanted to do this.

There was madness at work here and death wasn't the proper penalty. Ruff rolled to the right and peered out. Smoke still rose from the sage on the slope opposite.

Deliberately, wondering at his own sanity, he showed himself and then withdrew quickly as two more rounds were fired. And that—if the owner of that handgun had any sense—was the last round.

Ruff tested the theory cautiously, slowly showing himself again. He took one step down slope and the ambusher leaped up and started running south, still holding the empty gun.

Justice walked back to his horse and swung up. He started the black into a loping run. Ahead of him the ambusher ran, and Ruff saw wide eyes turned back toward him.

He measured his stride and kicked free of the stirrups. He was alongside the ambusher now and he simply stepped overboard, driving his adversary to the earth in a tumbling roll as the black ran on.

A solid right-hand blow to the jaw did the trick and Ruff stood up, wiping back his dark hair. The silver Colt lay on the ground beside his foot. Johnny Albright, Private, U.S. Army, lay crumpled against the earth.

Justice started walking after the black horse, tucking Rudy Stuyvestant's fancy Colt away behind his gunbelt. The black—damn him—had trampled over Ruff's hat and he picked it up and tried to reshape it. The black watched his approach with haughty eyes and blew with disgust.

By the time Ruff had ridden back, Johnny Albright was sitting up holding the back of his neck. His uniform was torn and dusty, his face coloring into a nice bruise.

"Why didn't you just shoot me? If you had to stop me, why didn't you just shoot me!"

"Why? What's your rush to die?" Ruff squatted down beside the kid.

"I deserve it. Why not? I stabbed Joe Gordon. All right. The army's going to kill me. All right." He still rubbed the back of his neck, youthful eyes lifting to Ruff's "If they don't kill me, I'm going to break rocks for ten years, all right?"

"So?"

"So! That's living death, Justice. I've heard the tales."

"It beats dying."

"In ten years . . ."

"You'll be a twenty-eight-year-old ex-soldier."

"No I won't. Don't kid me. In ten years I'll be ninety-nine. I once saw a man who did five years, Justice.

Gray, shrunken, hollow. He was up and moving around, Justice, shuffling around more like. All right? But he was dead. Plain dead. Why didn't you let me go?"

"And die out there?" Ruff looked southward.

"Yes. Isn't that what would happen?"

"Likely. Only you'd die bad, Johnny. You think the hard-labor camp is hell, you've no idea what a Cheyenne can do. Or have you heard those stories too?"

"I've heard 'em. So what."

"So nothing. I'll take you in and you'll tough it out or you won't."

"Joe Gordon is dying!"

"Then you'll hang."

"Justice . . ."

"I don't have a lot of choices, Johnny."

"No. I guess you don't." He hung his head. "You knew last night, didn't you? You knew that I was in that wagon."

"I could have guessed it. You were missing, needing a way out of Bismarck. You weren't in town anymore, where were you? Who took the gun when no one walked near the wagon? Had to be someone in the wagon."

"I thought you had it figured . . . why'd you let yourself get sucked into that fight?"

"He needed it."

"You wouldn't reconsider?" Albright asked.

"Letting you off here?"

"That's right."

"They'll find you, kid. No food, no gun, no horse— man, they'd find you before you were out of sight."

"Who says they're around?"

"They're around."

"They haven't bothered the wagon train."

"They've got forty guns to contend with there. But

they'll come anyway. They're biding their time, waiting for more warriors maybe. They'll come."

"Well, I guess I'm cooked, all right," Johnny Albright said with a little laugh.

"It looks like it."

"You understand, don't you, Justice? Understand what happened—how a man can hurt someone he don't mean to?"

"I understand. But you can't erase that stuff once it happens, my friend."

"Hanging me's not going to help Joe. Hell, he wouldn't even want me hung."

"No."

"But they're going to do it anyway." His eyes lifted to Ruff's again and a small smile lifted his mouth.

"Maybe not. You remember what I told you anyway. You're young enough, tough enough, to take ten years' hard if it comes to that."

"I ain't tough enough to take a broken neck."

And that was the last word on that. Justice didn't want to do it the way he did, but he wasn't going to take any foolish chances: he knotted a rope around John Albright's wrists and led him back to the wagon train on a tether.

They had halted for nooning, the oxen out of their yokes and grazing, the men around a hastily built, buffalo-dung-fueled campfire where coffee boiled. They stood and stared as Ruff rode up, walking the black through the camp until he found Rudy Stuyvestant, battered and swollen.

The kid was with his old man and held a shotgun. His eyes were not so eager and childlike as they had been the night before. He looked with scorn and hatred at Ruff. He was the sort to hold a long grudge, a killing grudge.

"What do you want?"

"It's Christmas." Ruff pulled the silver-mounted, pearl-handled Colt from behind his belt and tossed it at Rudy, who, unprepared, let it drop to the ground.

"Where did you get it? Who's that?" old man Stuyvestant growled.

Justice didn't answer. He walked the black forward and it shouldered the two men, father and son, aside. John Albright trailed silently after him as Ruff led the way toward the army noon fire.

Ruff didn't have to wait to clash with Lieutenant Ralston. The officer came around the corner of a wagon and started in.

"Where the hell have you been, Justice! I ordered you to ride—damn me," he said, pulling to a sudden verbal halt, "Johnny Albright."

The soldiers had gathered around. Ruff saw Reb Saunders glance at the kid and shrug. Sergeant Cornwall, appearing as blank and bland as always, ordered the kid untied.

"Where did you find him?" Ralston demanded.

"He slipped into the wagon back at Bismarck. After lifting Rudy Stuyvestant's gun, he waited for a chance to slide away. He tried it a few miles back. His tough luck I happened to be back there."

"Instead of ahead of us as you were told to be."

"That's right." Ruff yawned and that seemed to infuriate Ralston, but the sun was warm, and when a man wants to yawn, why he just does it. "I'd like to talk to you about something else," Justice said as Cornwall led John Albright away. The kid was beaten now, his head hanging to his chest.

"Is it important?"

"There's a lot you haven't been told about the gold-camp massacre," Ruff said honestly, "and I've come across something out there that you ought to know about."

The yellow eyes of Lieutenant Ralston flickered. "Let's talk then."

And they did, away from the fire where the soldiers drank their coffee, watching incuriously as the two men conferred.

"Ridiculous!"

Ruff agreed. "It is, the way it's told, but that doesn't alter the fact that men died out there. That someone is on our trail."

"I understood that you were a wild man, Justice, that you were considered unreliable. But I was also told that whatever you were, you knew this country, the Indian, tactics, and tracking. Now I doubt that. I'm starting to think you have some perverse sense of humor, that you are utterly irresponsible, that your chief objective in life is to stir up trouble and mock responsibility and duty."

Ruff Justice looked deeply into those topaz eyes for a long while. There was a lie lurking there, but he didn't know if it concerned him or someone, something, else. "I'll be out ahead of the train," he said. Then he turned and started walking away. The hand touched his shoulder and without looking back Ruff said, "You'd better be a hell of a lot better than Rudy Stuyvesant."

There was a second there when Ruff thought the hand wouldn't drop away, when he wondered how he was going to make a dollar after the army cut him loose for striking an officer.

But the hand did slide away, slowly, a greasy, dirty thing, and Ruff Justice walked away. He knew already, however. He couldn't have said how he knew it, but he did.

Before this was done he was going to have to kill Lieutenant Neil Ralston or be killed himself.

*   *   *

The wind was beginning to gust and there was an ominous grayness to the northern skies. The Heart River ran slate gray through its sandy channel. Ruff was a mile ahead of the wagon train, out of sight, out of hearing.

The gold camp was near the Little Heart fork and he wasn't far from there now. He wasn't far from it and he wasn't the only rider heading that way. She was back.

He had seen the unshod pony's tracks twice. And they were riding toward her favorite killing place.

There were forty men with guns in their party and the idea that a single girl could do them any harm was laughable. Ruff kept telling himself that.

And there were sixteen men in the Gates party. Sixteen. And all dead.

Ruff knew it was foolish, yet all the same he was wary and uncomfortable. What he saw next made him a hell of a lot more uncomfortable. He drew up sharply and sat looking, listening.

The Heart ran on, whispering, burbling, hissing, frothing white as it ran over the hidden rocks in its bed. Above, the gray wisps of cloud floated over. The wind talked in the willows.

There must have been at least thirty riders on the horses that had left their tracks on the sandy beach.

The black stood perfectly still. Ruff looked again at the sign, at the sandy, rising bluffs that fronted the river along this stretch, and then he turned his horse and got the hell out of there. He still had long hair and every intention of keeping it for a while longer.

He rode at an easy lope when he came in, but from time to time he glanced across his shoulder. Lieutenant Ralston was at the point of the patrol, Cornwall and a corporal Ruff didn't know flanking him.

"Ralston!"

The lieutenant, who liked being called "sir" by everyone, military personnel or not, flinched.

"What is it, Justice?"

"Better hold it up. There's Cheyenne sign ahead and plenty of it."

"What do you mean?"

Ruff looked to the placid Sergeant Cornwall and then to the skies. "I mean I found Cheyenne sign. Thirty men at least. They've got extra mounts with them. They crossed the Heart ahead of us less than a day ago. Moving south, toward the rendezvous they've made."

"That was supposed to be by the Tschida."

"Near it, by it. Barton wasn't that specific; he wasn't going to follow them to find out where they were going."

"The Tschida is west, not south."

"Ralston, dammit, we're riding into their teeth. I don't give a damn if they're meeting at Lake Tschida or in the Black Hills—they're ahead of us now. That's all I know. You want me to do my job, all right, I've done it. You've got hostiles ahead of you."

"They were ahead. You said they went past twenty-four hours ago."

Justice didn't even answer. His jaw was so tightly clenched he couldn't have. The man was determined to ride ahead to that gold camp. Was he that foolish? Did he believe that forty armed men would deter the Cheyenne in a war mood? Or was it the gold, the promise of it, that urged him on. Or the promise of Norah Gates.

"What do you recommend, scout?" Ralston asked stiffly.

"I recommend we veer north, get out onto the flats, away from the water and out of this area. Too many possibilities for ambush here."

"Naked female warriors, no doubt." Ralston lifted an eyebrow. He was enjoying it now. He glanced at Cornwall, who pretended to smile—the big sergeant had no real sense of humor at all, but he wanted to flatter the officer. "Is that it, Justice? Mr. Justice thinks we have an army of naked Amazons ahead of us, is that right, Justice! Answer me!"

"What I think we've got ahead is blood. What I think we've got is a body of men under the command of an incompetent officer. What I think we've got is a burial party looking for a place to happen."

"What is this?" Stuyvestant had ridden up from the wagons. Now he held back his frothing, rearing roan horse while he looked from Ralston to Ruff and back again. "What's the holdup? Trouble?"

"No trouble at all," Neil Ralston said. "Straight ahead, Stuyvestant. Keep them rolling."

Ruff turned his attention to Stuyvestant. He had the ability to turn this train if he wanted to, if he too wasn't as gold mad as Ralston seemed to be.

"The lieutenant doesn't think you need to know, Stuyvestant. I think you do. I rode over the sign of a Cheyenne war party. Large party. Thirty men at least, and probably others around nearby."

"Yeah? So what?" Stuyvestant spat.

"So what? You don't cherish that scalp of yours much, do you? This is no time to play games with me, Stuyvestant; it's not going to impress anyone."

"I'm not playing. You say thirty men. All right. I've got forty and they're all good fighting men. They've all got repeating rifles and six-guns. The Indians know that."

"Yes, and there was a time when it meant something, when half a dozen whites could hold back an army of hostiles, but not anymore. They've got weapons as good as yours, likely, and they know the terrain, tactics like your men couldn't."

"Hear that, Ralston? Damned army don't know tactics." Stuyvestant guffawed and spat again. "What is it, Justice, don't you want anyone else riding into that gold camp? Figure on picking up that dust for yourself, do you?"

"No one knows there's any dust there for one thing, not any longer. No, I don't want the gold. I want my hair, and I want the woman safe. On top of that, I don't want it said that I led a cavalry unit and a party of civilians into a slaughter."

"Oh, he's worried about his reputation!"

"And your butt. You don't seem to be worried about it."

"I'm not playing, Justice!" Stuyvestant roared. "I've got Lieutenant Ralston here to make decisions. If I don't like what he decides, I've got my own head. I don't need some long-haired monkey guiding me. If the army don't trust you, why in hell should I?"

"Let me take the woman north."

"Do you think she'll go?" Stuyvestant sneered.

"She might, if she understood."

"Ask her. I don't give a damn. I didn't invite her on this train, she came of her own accord. She can leave when she wants to."

"Justice, you'll not ride off from this column with that woman," Ralston said.

"Stop me."

Ruff turned his black and held up at the side of the trail waiting for Norah's wagon, which was being driven by a hired man. The cavalry was out a little distance on either flank. Stuyvestant's men were bunched in closer.

The party looked formidable, but Ruff saw only weaknesses as he looked it over now—heavy, immobile wagons, inexperienced warriors riding horses not trained for battle, an inept, inexperienced officer leading the army forces, and all-around good cover for an attacking force.

"Norah."

He rode up beside her wagon and she leaned out. She wore a gray bonnet with a bright green ribbon, a white blouse and sealskin jacket, and a gray skirt.

"What is it, Ruff?"

"There's Indian sign ahead of us. A lot of it. I don't think you ought to be here."

"No?" She laughed. "And what should I do, go back?"

"Ride out with me. We'll circle around. We've got to get away from the Heart. They're bound to haunt this area for water."

"But I'm going to the gold camp! How can I ride off? And where would we go?"

"To Morgan Creek. You can rejoin the wagon train there and they'll take you back to Bismarck."

"I don't want to go to Morgan Creek, Ruff, you know that! I want the gold that's mine. I need it!"

"I want you to live. That's more important, don't you think?"

"Without the gold . . . Ruff, it wouldn't be much of a living, would it? I've got debts at home, I told you. I've got a mother I have to take care of—and it takes money to do that!"

"You won't consider it?"

"You know I can't." She shook her head. "I just can't."

Then that was that. No one was willing to consider living, not when there was a chance they could die rich. The skies were going gray. It would rain. The river swept past and the wagon train rolled on, straight toward the Heart River gold camp and its bloody memories.

And out there somewhere the Cheyenne would be watching.

8.

The night camp was silent. Maybe no one was willing to follow Justice's advice, but they knew now that they were in Indian country. There was none of that joking around the campfire and there were fewer people in camp, more posted as sentries.

The men were never far from their weapons. They looked up from their fires as Ruff Justice walked past and there was something bitter and accusing in their eyes, as if they blamed him for bringing the Cheyenne near.

"Why, Mr. Justice, have yourself a cup of coffee," Reb Saunders said. "I thought you'd be off somewhere with a Spanish dancing lady or something." Reb grinned and poured Justice a cup of coffee. The soldiers around the fire leaned in a little closer. They knew about the trouble between Ralston and Justice. They didn't know the cause of it. Justice hadn't told anyone yet about Lieutenant Neil Ralston and the Chinese girl.

"Thanks, Reb. What about him?"

Ruff lifted his chin toward the man who sat nearby, hands and feet tied, head hanging, youthful face drawn and dusty. The eyes of Johnny Albright lifted to Justice. There wasn't even recognition in them. Albright was living through his own private hell.

"I give him some earlier," Reb said. "He didn't touch it."

"Poor bastard."

"That touches it," Reb agreed. He sipped at his own coffee, watching the lean man in buckskins across the fire. "Is it bad, Ruff?"

"It won't go, me telling the enlisted men about the Indians, Reb." Ruff shook his head. "What you've heard is probably true, but you know I can't incite you boys against the officers."

"Is that what it would be if you told me what was happening, Ruff? Inciting us?"

"I guess that's exactly what it would be, Reb," Ruff answered quietly. Every man around that fire knew that he had just been warned to keep his eyes open and his powder dry. They all knew that there was big trouble over the rise and there was nothing in the world Ruff Justice could do to help them out of it.

"Sorry, I don't feel much like singing or jawing, boys," Ruff said. They nodded and Ruff got up. He walked to where Johnny Albright sat tied.

He crouched down and checked the kid's hands, seeing that they had color in them. "You all right, Albright?"

"I reckon," he answered with a voice as creaky as a rusty gate.

"Want anything?"

"No. I don't want anything."

Justice put a hand briefly on the kid's shoulder and then rose.

"Justice," Albright said, "I don't hold no grudge."

"I hoped not."

"Hell, maybe I'll get away again, huh?" He tried to smile but it didn't work out well.

"Probably will."

"I wonder how Joe Gordon is tonight."

No one knew the answer to that. The young soldier who had taken a knife in the liver was alive or dead.

They wouldn't know for a week or more. Ruff could look at the kid and almost wish he had gotten away, that he had let him go. Almost. Because there is such a thing as responsibility. Albright had stabbed a man. Ruined him for life possibly, possibly killed him. All for nothing. Albright owed, it was that simple.

It didn't keep Justice from feeling sorry for the man.

He slept alone, away from the camp, back among a stand of huge white oaks, hearing the river run, the wind in the trees, the occasional grumbling of distant thunder. The moon floated high through the shifting clouds, silvering them, and far away the coyote howled.

The dawn was a gray, cold thing creeping out of the east. Rain drizzled down out of the lowering skies. The black horse was slick with moisture when Ruff saddled up and rode out without speaking to anyone, without eating.

A mile down the trail he felt more comfortable, even with the cold and the rain. The horse had loosened up, its muscles warming, and it moved evenly along the river road—nothing more than a narrow ribbon of sandy beach, which the wagons of Stuyvestant would be able to follow so long as the river didn't rise.

And when it did rise—well, they would be stuck and that would just be that.

It was noon when he found the camp. It was a long while before he could bring himself to cross the river and ride through the willows, the willows Barton McGinnis had found Tug Gates lying in, his body crippled, helpless.

Justice let the black find its own ford. A crow dipped low, flying through the rain toward some uncertain goal, cawing loudly.

The willows were silver with water. The gold camp was just as Barton had described it. Ruff sat the black for a long while before swinging down, rifle in his hand, to stride through the rain toward the circle of skulls.

Until that moment he really hadn't believed it. He had no reason to doubt Bart, but it was a thing that wasn't accepted easily. The evidence, irrefutable, sat there now. Empty skulls stared at Ruff Justice from stakes driven into the soft earth. Ruff's mouth tightened. He glanced around—there were no bodies, just the skulls. Old bedrolls lay moldering in the rain; tools coated now with rust lay scattered around.

The sound of approaching horses brought Ruff's head around. He automatically lifted his Spencer .56 as he moved. There were six of them. The man in front wore a blue uniform.

"What are you up to, Justice?" Ralston demanded.

"Simple," Stuyvestant replied. "He wanted to get here first, didn't you, Justice?"

"That's what I understood my job to be," Ruff said. He lowered his rifle, letting it rest casually in the crook of his arm.

Ralston was there and with him two soldiers: Cornwall and that hard-looking corporal Ruff didn't know. Stuyvestant had Rudy with him. And then there was Norah, her face flushed, her eyes bright, her bonnet dripping rain. She rode her horse astraddle. She had somewhere gotten a pair of men's twill pants which she had rolled up and belted tightly. They didn't fit but just now Norah didn't give a damn how she looked, apparently.

"Did you find it?" she asked breathlessly. She slid from her horse and rushed to Justice. She looked with a questioning gaze into his blue, cold eyes. "Did you find it?" she repeated.

"I haven't looked."

She whispered quickly in his ear. "Don't forget what

you promised. They'll take the gold if you let them. I'll be good to you, I swear it."

Her breath was warm, misty, pleasant against his ear; but it gave Justice a cold chill somehow. Greed frequently had that effect on him, and that was what he was seeing—greed in her green eyes, greed in the somber expression of Stuyvestant, greed in the hard, steely glare of Lieutenant Ralston. Or in Ralston's case it might have been more than greed. His eyes combed Norah Gates inch by inch, measuring her, and he had decided apparently that she suited his purposes very well indeed.

"Well?" Norah asked. She had stepped back, trying vainly to indicate that she had said nothing to Justice, that her only interest in the events around her was casual. It was that—very casual. For a woman who fainted at the mention of death, Norah hadn't been much affected by the sight of sixteen skulls staring at her.

Ralston had swung down, giving his reins to his corporal. Stuyvestant and Rudy were also on the ground now, looking around through the gray haze with great interest. Rudy, Justice thought, looked a little wary at least. He glanced from time to time at the skulls, then looked quickly away.

"He hasn't had time to go through their bedrolls," Rudy said.

"No. Let's have at it," his father replied.

"Hold on, that's not your gold, is it?" Ruff objected.

"It's mine if I find it."

"It belongs to the survivors of these men."

"What men? Who the hell are they?" Stuyvestant asked, waving a hand toward the skulls. "Are you prepared to identify these bodies?"

Norah looked at Ruff in panic. So that was their idea. Who could identify these men? Even Tug Gates—

although Bart had said he saw Tug here, Barton McGinnis didn't know with any certainty that Tug had gold dust with him.

"The army will take charge of any gold that is found," Ralston chipped in, playing his trump card. "Until a court can settle the matter of ownership."

"We haven't found anything yet," Ruff reminded them all.

"But it's mine," Norah said. She was very good at tragedy, Ruff decided. Lord, she was beautiful, this honey-haired, green-eyed woman. She was beautiful and desirable and very deadly. Justice was certain of that now. She was not a woman to lie down with—you just might not get up again.

"It's my gold, Justice!" she said frantically.

"Let's find your brother's roll if we can. It could be he'll have had a letter with his name on it, other papers that will prove the roll and any dust in it was his."

If there was any doubt that there was gold in the camp, it was dispelled immediately by Rudy Stuyvesant, who let out a war whoop of satisfaction.

"Gold. Damn me, it's gold! Look here, Pa."

A sack of dust had been lying smack in the middle of the clearing. Rudy swooped down on it and snatched it up. It was an Easter egg hunt for big boys. Rudy lifted the sack of dust and waved it in the air.

"Keep looking," Stuyvestant shouted.

Ralston had gotten into the act, and even the phlegmatic Cornwall. They were tearing apart the bedrolls of the dead men. Norah was frantically digging through an insect-infested, weather-rotted pack.

Justice stood and watched them, his rifle cradled in his arms. He stood and watched them as did the jeering dead. The skulls of those who had already learned their lesson—that it wasn't worth dying for.

"It's here. It's here!" Norah was on her hands and knees, yanking sack after sack from the pack she was digging through. Small chamois sacks filled with heavy, metallic dust. She was breathing through her mouth, panting as she ripped at the rotten cloth.

"Is it your brother's?" Ruff asked.

"It's here. It's mine, do you hear!" She spun toward Ruff, her blond hair hanging in damp strands across her eyes, her hands muddy and clawlike. "It's all mine. You keep away from it!"

Ruff Justice turned and walked away. If there was anything to be found, they would find it.

He stood for a time watching the river run, hearing the occasional chirp of surprise and satisfaction as someone behind him found another cache of dust. No one had mentioned burying what there was of the dead, and he didn't care to do it himself. It seemed more fitting somehow that the skulls should sit glowering at the looters.

Ruff walked across the camp and into the willows, looking for the spot where Bart had found Tug Gates. If the body was still there, it might bear proof that the assumed identity was correct, that Norah had the right to some of that dust. No matter how he was beginning to feel about the woman, he wanted her to have that gold if she had the right.

Search as he might, he couldn't find a sign of Tug Gates's body, however, or of a gun, clothing, saddle, or personal belongings of any kind.

What he found were the pony tracks.

They emerged from the river and then led off toward the south, and as Justice followed them it became obvious that the rider was moving in a circle around the camp.

The tracks were less than an hour old. The woman was back, riding her circle of death.

The rain continued, increasing as the day wore on. Ruff walked back to the camp and found the spoilers busy with their take. Most of the gold had been piled into a neat stack, though Rudy Stuyvestant stood to one side with two small sacks in one hand and a look in his eye that challenged anyone to try to take it away from him.

"Ruff!" Norah rushed up to him as he approached through the cold rain. "They won't let me have it. They say it's theirs."

Her hands clutched at him. Her body was near and promising. Could she need the gold that badly?

"I simply told her that the army is confiscating all of the gold until the courts can make a decision," Ralston said severely, "and if you don't like it, Justice . . ."

"I haven't got anything to do with it, I'm afraid," Ruff answered, and Norah, who had been clinging to him, now fell away, her eyes harsh and astonished.

"You promised!"

"No one has taken your money. Isn't that so, Ralston?"

The lieutenant answered too quickly, too insincerely. "Of course, Justice, of course."

"Rudy—maybe you'd better toss what you have onto the pile," Ruff suggested.

"You can go to hell. I found it."

"Yeah, but it's not yours, is it, Ralston? No one owns any portion of this gold until the courts have taken it under consideration. That's what the lieutenant said, isn't it?"

"Yeah," the kid said sullenly. He tossed his sacks onto the pile of gold dust. "I guess that's right."

Don't turn your back on him, Justice reminded himself. That's twice you've straightened the kid up and he'll remember it. He'll remember.

Ruff looked up toward the Heart. Through the rain the main party was approaching, the wagons creeping heavily along the sandy beach.

"Hell of a place to camp," Ruff told Ralston. The lieutenant's yellow eyes glittered like gold in a dark pool of water as he turned them to Ruff.

"It'll do."

"It didn't do for the prospectors. Look, Ralston, use some common sense. If this rain doesn't stop, we're going to be virtually trapped here. High water on one side, the bluffs behind us. That leaves no way out, especially for the wagons."

"What is it with you, Justice? Why do you want us to go north? You figure there's a big cache of gold here somewhere? Bigger than anything we've turned up yet?" Ralston smiled crookedly, as if they shared a dirty secret.

"I figure we're going to get scalped if we don't clear off, is what I figure."

"Sure. By naked women. All right, I could use some of that scalping."

"Like in Minneapolis?"

"Shut up about that!" Ralston stiffened with rage. "Who have you told about that? It was nothing anyway. Some chink girl. Maybe I got a little too rough, maybe—"

"I was there, Ralston, remember?"

"Yeah. I remember. You remember this: I'm in charge of this party and we'll move when I say to, we'll ride *where* I say we ride. Remember one other thing: there are ways an officer can take care of an uncooperative civilian scout."

"Are there? I'm a man, Ralston, not a woman. You'd have a little trouble beating me."

Ralston stood there in the rain, his jaw working soundlessly, his fists clenched. Ruff had gone too far and he knew it. He almost wished he had kept his mouth shut. This wasn't gaining him anything. The whole objective was to get these people through to Morgan Creek alive. For the rest of it he didn't give a damn. And what he had just done hadn't contributed a lot to a solution. He had Ralston dead set against him now. Any suggestion was going to be automatically rejected.

The rain fell. The river, gray and frothing, rambled past, rising to cut off the sandy bar where the gold camp had been. Ralston had his mind only on gold. The soldiers set up a haphazard camp as the wagoneers unhitched their oxen. Ruff looked around one more time and slowly, profusely, cursed the day, the weather, and Ralston. If the Cheyenne came, they were dead, all of them.

And the Cheyenne would come.

9.

The rain hissed down, driven by the night wind. Below, the camp slept or tossed fitfully, dreaming of golden riches. Ruff Justice sat awake on the bluff above and behind the gold camp, his groundsheet propped up on two sticks to serve as a shelter against the rain. He had his blanket around his shoulders, his rifle on his lap. He was brooding darkly, liking not a bit of this, unable to do anything about it.

He should have turned Ralston in to MacEnroe at first sight. The old man might not have done anything, but then again he might have. Norah Gates. He should have refused to guide for them while they had a woman along. She was beautiful, enough so to make a man lose a part of his reason. But she was a deadly thing.

He wondered how Johnny Albright was making it on this night. He and Albright had something in common now. They were both prisoners. Justice was hostage to his own folly, he felt, and it angered him. . . .

What was that?

He stiffened and stared out against the night and rain, seeing the clouds crawl across the velvet plains, seeing the river run. Nothing. He couldn't make out a thing and so he settled back, not quite relaxing, but letting the tension go out of his muscles, breathing more slowly. Only his eyes did not relax.

They were out there—or someone was, some thing.

Lightning flickered dully among the rolling clouds and faint thunder followed. It flashed again, nearer, scoring the rain with silver-white light.

And by that light Ruff saw her. East of the camp, riding through the rain, dark horse, dark figure. A lone riding woman.

The lightning burned itself out fitfully and she was gone. If she was ever there, Ruff thought. Maybe imagination was beginning to boggle his thoughts. It could have been nothing but a cavalryman on sentry duty. But Ruff had seen them go out and they had gone afoot.

He tossed his blanket aside. He rose to his feet and went out into the rain, slipping into a black rain slicker as he made his way toward his horse.

He was tired of this mystery. He didn't like not knowing what was going on around him. He meant to find out just who or what this lone rider was . . . even if it cost him his head.

The black horse looked up at him dismally. Water glossed its dark coat. Ruff saddled in the darkness and walked the animal down the slanting bluff to the flats east of the gold camp. Then he began his stalking.

He rode through the rain and the night, no more than a shadow himself in his slicker, on the dark horse. The wind was gusting heavily now, throwing handfuls of rain against him, stinging his face and hands. He crossed the Little Heart, which was not running deep—its channel was too shallow for that—but wide, spread out across the bottomland. Beyond that was the broken country where he had seen the lone rider.

Justice walked the horse out of the river and started up the narrow arroyo beyond. Lightning flashed again, striking nearby. The Cheyenne warrior leaped from the rocks above him and together they tumbled down the arroyo as thunder rumbled mockingly and the silver knife in the hand of the Cheyenne brave flashed downward.

They hit the ground hard. Ruff's black had skidded back and now, after rearing up in panic and confusion, it trampled on its own reins, trying to get away from the struggling men nearly beneath it.

Water rushed down the shallow arroyo. It was cold beneath Ruff's back. But he wasn't paying a whole lot of attention to that just then.

The Cheyenne had leaped from the rocks and collided solidly with him. Together they had hit the ground, the Cheyenne trying to rip his throat open with his hunting knife. Ruff managed to get a blocking hand up, and as the Indian's knife drove downward, his wrist caught Ruff's forearm, thwarting the blow.

Ruff drove a knee up and the Indian grunted with pain. It didn't stop the Cheyenne from trying again with the knife. But Justice had him with both hands at the wrist and the Cheyenne, kicking wildly, rolling and thrashing, couldn't get the hand free.

Nor could Ruff reach his own weapons. He cursed the confining rain slicker, which denied him the chance to get the bowie hanging from his belt or the big Colt opposite it.

There were two men there in the night storm. Two men with one weapon, and whoever had that knife was going to survive. The one without it was going to die.

Ruff drove his forehead into the Cheyenne's nose and hot blood spurted onto his own face. As he felt the Indian sag he exerted pressure on the hand holding the razor-edged knife. He folded the hand back on itself until the fingers inexorably opened and the knife dropped free.

Lightning flickered again and Justice was looking

directly into a dark, yellow-painted face, a face smeared with blood and earth. Grappling hands searched for the knife and Ruff Justice found it first.

He grabbed the Indian by the back of his head, wrapping his fingers in his dark hair. Then yanking back, exposing the throat, he struck home with the knife. The Cheyenne writhed for a time, but he was dead as soon as the knife edge pierced his throat. He died in Ruff's arms.

A long minute passed before Justice rose. He lay there feeling the cold rain mingle with the hot blood of a man who no longer lived. Then he rolled the Cheyenne aside and got shakily to his feet.

"Damn you," he said. The black horse had trotted off and left him afoot. It had never done that before, although it had smelled Indians before, smelled human blood, and seen savagery. He started after it, throwing the Indian's knife down, unbuttoning his slicker as he went. His rifle he found at the bottom of the arroyo, and snatching it up, he hurried on.

He was hurrying now with reason. That Cheyenne wasn't here hanging around the gold camp because he liked sitting in the rain. Something was brewing, and when he had attacked Ruff, he had proven it. There was no real need for it, unless he was afraid that Justice would find him—or a larger party of Cheyenne—first.

It looked like, it smelled like, war.

The black horse stood near the river, looking toward Justice and then toward the water. The Little Heart boiled past now, shallow and swift, white and deep cobalt.

"Damn you," Ruff muttered again. Then he calmed himself. Maybe the horse was sensing his anger.

Or perhaps he sensed what Justice didn't: the presence of another enemy behind him.

The lone rider came out of the darkness and the horse was nearly on top of Justice before he heard the drumming of hooves and threw himself violently to one side, rolling away as the horse thundered past.

It was dark as sin and the rain was falling down, but still Justice saw, even as he rolled. He saw that it was a woman. Barton McGinnis hadn't been mistaken at all.

She wore a shirt on this rainy night, but her hair, soaked and long, was worn free. She was young—that was the only impression he had as to her looks. A lone woman riding on this night. A lone woman who killed. Who killed and then mutilated, who made mystic gestures.

He got to his feet and staggered toward the bluffs. She was coming back. He wasn't going to dodge the horse and he knew it. Justice braced himself.

He looked up, saw the long hair flying, saw the white of teeth, saw the glint in the horse's eye, saw the paint on the animal's neck.

Justice felt the hard impact of the horse's shoulder, and as he was jolted he grabbed the left forefoot of the Indian pony, forcing it back. When the horse tried to place its foot, it missed, landed on its knee, and rolled.

Hooves cut near Justice's head as he flattened himself against the sandy beach. The woman went flying. The silver rain drove down and the horse, finishing its roll, landed hard on its side and thrashed as it came to its feet, leaving the rider's blanket behind.

The woman tried to rise but Justice, bruised and angry, was first up. She got to one knee and started away but Ruff hurled himself through the air and caught her at the waist, driving her down.

He landed on top of her and pinioned her by going astraddle, his knees on her arms as he looked down into the young, dark, quite pretty face of a woman.

"God loves you, brother," she gasped.

Ruff Justice had his bowie in his hand. His teeth were bared in a savage grimace. His hair hung dark and long. His hand was on her throat, and he had been ready to do the deed. He hadn't been brought up to hurt women, but in this country a man learned a she-wolf was as dangerous as any, and this woman had done sixteen men to death.

"God loves you, brother," she panted again, and Ruff slackened his grip slightly.

"What do you want? Who are you? Where are the warriors?" he demanded.

"I think . . ." she began, but it was then that the first of the shots rang out. Shots and then screaming sounded above the hiss and rumble of storm, and then bright fire shone against the gray of night. Ruff slammed his fist against the girl's jaw, bound her quickly with his scarf and a strip cut from her saddle blanket, dragged her into a shallow wash, and left her there.

Then, snatching up the reins to his black horse, he splashed across the river again, riding hell for it toward the gold camp, where fierce fighting had broken out.

The horse kicked up fans of icy water. The rain drummed down. Justice heeled the black savagely, but it did no good. The animal could run no faster than it could run.

He was still half a mile from the camp when he realized the shots were dying down, the flames increasing—that would be the wagons, he knew, stripped of their goods and torched. And if the Cheyenne had been able to loot and torch the wagons, then they had won the battle. Won it quickly, decisively.

And why not? The army slept, the teamsters slept. There had been only a few guards out, and these would have been no match for the Cheyenne infiltrators slinking through the stormy night.

Justice rode up the sandy bluff, and as his horse slackened its pace, bogged down in the tough going, he leaped down and led it on.

Norah Gates. He knew they had her and the idea sent hot rage creeping through his arteries. He had met people from the East before who had laughed at the idea of a woman taking the last bullet before allowing an Indian to capture her. But then they had never seen a woman raped to death, her womb torn open. They had never seen what a band of Indian squaws could do to a captive. They reveled in torture, did the women. Yes, there was a savagery in the Indian, a savagery those who knew him only through books would never know. Justice had seen it. Justice hoped Norah Gates had taken the last bullet.

He crested the bluff near his own tiny camp and saw the fire painting wild images against the shifting mirror of the rain. He bellied up to the crest of the bluff, leaving the weary black horse below, out of sight.

"Quite right." Justice bit at the inside of his mouth. Everything he had suspected from the day he had seen the first Cheyenne sign had happened. He was a seer, the greatest prognosticator since Nostradamus.

It didn't do a damn bit of good to see the future if you couldn't change it. The dead lay on the field below and nothing Justice had forecast had done any good. He could see the soldiers, some in their long johns, some in half a uniform, bootless or nearly naked, lying dead across the sandy beach. The Cheyenne walked among them, taking whatever item of clothing appealed to them.

Farther back the wagons blazed gloriously, weaving

red and yellow flames dancing into the night sky
while the cold rain fell into the rushing, roiling Heart.

He couldn't see Norah. He couldn't find Ralston,
although he doubted he could identify the officer's
body at this distance, under these conditions.

He couldn't identify anyone at all, but he thought
he saw Cornwall's round body and possibly Corporal
Gray, twisted, bloody. He had to content himself with
a body count. The sort of report Colonel MacEnroe
loved. They could say anything they wanted about the
old man—except that he didn't care about casualties.
He did care, desperately. Ruff had been with him the
night the colonel drank himself into insensibility after the Thorn Creek massacre.

Ruff eased away from the scene below him. There
were, by rough count, thirty dead whites, fifty Cheyenne warriors very much alive, wildly celebrating—
they had found the whiskey Stuyvestant had been
taking to the Morgan Creek mining community.

But where was Norah?

Where was Norah and where was Ralston? Dead,
perhaps, and carried away. But Justice didn't think so.
Even if he had no rational reason for believing as he
did.

"Sure, they took her. Why not?"

They took her to their war camp. Any other prisoners would have gone there as well. Unless they were
going to skin their heads and . . . the woman would
know.

She would know where the camp was and she was
going to talk. She spoke English, enough to say, "God
loves you, brother," and that meant she knew enough
to guide Justice to the war camp.

The war camp's location had suddenly become
essential. Even if Ralston was dead, if Norah was
dead, there was still a large threat of war looming on

the plains, and MacEnroe had to be informed. He had to know where the enemy was meeting, or those who had died in the gold camp wouldn't be the last.

He walked the black slowly down the slope, moving silently. Then he was aboard and across the Little Heart again as the moon appeared briefly through the cold, ragged clouds. It silvered the river before the storm closed out the Cheyenne moon once more.

He found her where he had left her.

Ruff swung down and trotted to her. She opened her mouth to speak, to scream, but he had taken the scarf from her feet and now he jammed it into her mouth. He couldn't have any noise, not now. Not here.

He threw her over the withers of the black and swung up himself, heeling the big horse up the bluffs and away from the river, riding blindly through the storm, leading her pony.

He held the woman down. It was uncomfortable as hell for her, he knew, but then it had been uncomfortable for the men whose heads she had gleefully skinned.

The storm seemed to be lifting. The moon again shone briefly through the clouds and by that light Justice was able to get his bearings. He knew where he wanted to go, to the large stand of oaks atop the crooked ridge he had passed that morning. There he would have cover and high ground. He would be near the gold camp yet out of sight and sound.

He rode up along the muddy flank of the ridge and entered the oaks where all seemed cool and dark and devoid of living things. The moon glossed the trunks of the oaks.

"Here," Ruff said to himself, to the horse, and the captive woman.

He swung down and grabbed the woman's bound arms, dragging her after him. He saw her eyes, wide and questioning. He didn't feel a lot of pity for her. She had done too much.

Ruff half carried, half dragged her into the deep copse where scrub oak and sycamores crowded the dark giant trees.

He sat her against the large oak and pulled the gag from her mouth.

"Thank you, Christian brother," the girl said, and Ruff snorted derisively.

"Christian brother, is it? Do you know what's happened tonight?"

"A very bad massacre," she said. She understood English perfectly well, and she spoke it in the mission-school fashion, in that way some Indians had learned that made it seem they were going to break into a hymn at any moment.

"You are Cheyenne. Where's your war camp?"

"Not far."

"Where!" Justice said roughly.

"Not far. You will be hurt if you go there."

"Yes, and those who have been taken there will be hurt."

"Yes," she said readily.

"Who is the war leader of this party?"

"I do not know."

"The *war leader*." Ruff repeated it in the Cheyenne tongue and the girl nodded rapidly.

"Yes. Eagle Spirit."

"I haven't heard the name," he said, mostly to himself. "What is he, a sachem? Shaman, maybe?"

"Shaman, yes," she said.

Not a hereditary chief or a man who had earned his position through bravery, but a man who counted on magic or supposed magic for his strength. These times things were desperate enough with the Indian that a lot of charlatans had sprung up among them, ghost dancers who promised to drive the white man out of their land, strange shamans with strange creeds and rituals, white-buffalo magic and cloaks of invisibility, magic bullets.

"Down!" Ruff hissed it. He took the girl and pressed her against the muddy earth. He could hear the horses walking past, see suddenly the dark figures against the sky as the warriors passed. Ten, a dozen, more.

Ruff had one hand on the girl's mouth, one hand on his rifle. If she tried to, she could scream, however. And if she screamed, it was all over. He pulled his bowie softly from his sheath and put it against her throat, warning her silently.

She believed he would do it. Her own people would have done it. Ruff could see her eyes, wide and dark by the starlight, which shone feebly through the rifts in the clouds. The horsemen passed and then were gone. Ten minutes later Ruff loosened his grip and pulled the knife away.

"Where are they riding?" he asked. "The home camp?"

"Yes, the home camp. In the hills."

"The camp is by the Tschida," Ruff said.

"No. It is not, I swear it."

"All right." He sat back on his haunches, looking at his prisoner. What use was she to him? The best thing that could have happened would have been for her to break her neck in that fall.

He asked her, "How many warriors in your camp?"

"Maybe three hundred, maybe four hundred."

"Damn," Ruff said softly. What then? Ride for Lincoln? By the time they could get back, there sure as hell wouldn't be any prisoners alive—if they were alive now. But they must be. They wouldn't have captured them and then taken them somewhere else to be killed. Or would they? It would be crazy. But then again maybe that was what Ruff was dealing with—madness, racial anger, hatred, religious fanatics. War parties didn't generally hold prisoners. If they could be used to work for the tribe, yes. As slaves for the women, perhaps; but the war party had no women with it. Save one.

"Eagle Spirit," he said, and the girl looked at him intently. "Is he . . ." Ruff touched his temple. The girl turned her eyes down.

"He is bad. He is too crazy for his blood. He is a madman."

"Then what are you doing with him? What are you doing with the war party anyway?"

"He is my brother."

"Eagle Spirit?"

"Yes. My brother. Part a brother. My father had two wives."

"I see." Ruff looked around. "We can't stay here. Get up. We're moving."

"But where do we go?"

Where, indeed. Ruff Justice had no idea. The country was crawling with hostile Indians. The gold camp by pure chance had been established a stone's throw from the biggest war camp in months. And Ralston out of greed, Stuyvestant out of the same motive, had brought their people smack into it. Now there were a lot of dead soldiers and teamsters back there along the Heart. And somewhere ahead a very live, quite mad ghost dancer named Eagle Spirit who was ready to sweep across the plains, beginning a war of retribution that would stain the prairie red.

Against that army stood Ruff Justice alone, and even to Ruff the odds seemed just a little long as he helped the Cheyenne girl to her feet and stood there in the dark and rain, cursing the savage night.

10.

It was still raining at dawn when Ruff stood in the shelter of the oaks to the south of the gold camp, less than a mile from the Cheyenne position. He could see the fires burning in their camp, like drops of flame that had fallen from the crimson sun, which bled through the long strands of clouds.

"Are your friends there?" the girl asked.

"My friends? Yes," he answered, not bothering to go into the finer points. Friends was a good-enough word.

"They will be kept until tonight. Tonight is the magic night. Other warriors will come to see if Eagle Spirit is what he says."

"He'll show them the white hostages to prove that he's a strong warrior." Yes, that would be it. Especially the soldiers—that was always a coup, to take a yellow leg.

"And then he will kill them. With magic, perhaps."

The girl was so calm about it that it riled Ruff briefly. He turned to look at her. Her buckskins were as wet as his own, clinging to a robust, healthy figure. The girl had lived an athlete's life, and it had suited her.

Her teeth were even and very white against the mahogany of her face. Her ears were small, her eyes wide, her nose narrow and slightly arched.

"What are you doing here?" Ruff asked, going nearer,

towering over her. "What are you doing here at all, woman? Who have you killed? What is your magic?"

"My magic is the Lord," she said.

"What?"

"My magic is the Lord, brother."

"I don't understand you. Where did you learn your English?"

"On the reservation. For a time we were on the big reservation."

"But you broke out."

"My brother killed some white men and we left." She shrugged. "I am not happy since."

"You liked the reservation?"

"Sometimes. I liked the church, the father. He taught me to praise the Lord."

Ruff looked at her closely, not quite sure she was serious. She might just be trying to prove she was a tame Indian, unlike her brother.

"I saw your pony's tracks far back, near the Missouri River," he told her. "You followed the wagons."

"I saw more people coming out here and I wanted to warn you that my brother would kill you all."

"But you didn't."

"I was frightened after all. I could not do it."

Ruff nodded. Maybe. No one would have listened to her anyway. "What about the gold camp?"

"What?"

"The camp on the Heart. You were there. Not tonight, but before. You were seen, riding around the camp, carrying a dead man's head. You killed those men."

"I do not kill them!" she said hotly. "I am not a sinner."

"No? What happened, then?" The sun was warm on Ruff's back now. The girl, eyes wide and sincere, was a step away from him. She bit at her lip then nodded her head sharply as if she had made up her mind to something.

"Eagle Spirit killed them."

"All of them?"

"Yes."

"One at a time?"

"Yes," the girl answered. "To frighten them all. To do magic through their fear. No one could leave the camp. Eagle Spirit had his men all around it. If they left, they were taken back. Dead. If they stayed, they died. Eagle Spirit crept in at night and made his magic—"

"Killed them, you mean?"

"Yes. Eagle Spirit did not listen to the white priests."

"No, I didn't think so," Ruff said dryly. His finger lifted her chin. "But you are the one that was seen. Just you."

"No! Eagle Spirit was seen," she argued.

"Yes?"

"Yes, of course. The dead saw him."

You couldn't argue that. "But the last man saw you. Riding in a circle around the camp. Then a man in buckskins saw you."

"Yes. A skinny man in buckskins." She nodded happily, as if that supported her innocence.

"Why don't you tell me what happened. What you were doing there at all." Ruff stripped off his shirt to hang it on the limb of the oak, to let the wind and meager sunlight dry it. The girl did the same.

If the priests had taught her anything, it hadn't been modesty. She had just pulled her shirt up over her head and hung it beside Ruff's. Nice. They were very nice. Young, pert, full, uptilted breasts with dark, erect nipples.

The girl turned toward him. "What is wrong?"

"Nothing. Women in your tribe take their clothes off in front of strangers now?"

"It is all right. You are a white man."

"What?"

"You are a white man. The father told me that it was all right for me to undress in front of white men. That is not wrong."

"I see."

"There *is* something wrong?"

"I just wouldn't make a habit of it," Ruff told her. He shifted his eyes away from her body. "Tell me the whole thing now." He walked to his horse and unsaddled as she spoke. The morning was cold. The girl crossed her arms over her breasts and spoke as Ruff worked.

"I came south with my brother to save him from killing. Killing is wrong. And this is Eagle Spirit's wish: to kill all the white men." She stepped back as Ruff swung his saddle to the ground, whisked off the blanket, and placed it on the tree branch.

"Go on."

"A spirit told my brother to come to these hills. So he says—I do not believe in this spirit, but my brother does. Or he says so. He tells everyone it is very strong. And so we came to these hills. Along the way we passed white settlements. Eagle Spirit burned their houses and killed the people. Then he told me that the spirit who guided him had given him instructions—to kill in a certain way that would be a sign. He began to kill certain people in this way."

"Peeling the hide from their skulls?"

"Just so. And making the magic circle. Strength is in the circle because it is eternal. So the spirit told my brother. The priest told me: 'The circle is eternal. Hatred is a circle. We must love.' So I told my brother. He laughed."

Ruff silently agreed. Hatred is a circle. War and hatred, one side trying to even it up against the other endlessly. He slipped the bit from the black's mouth, rubbed the horse a little with a handful of grass, and hobbled it.

"So you came south with your brother and he killed the men in the gold camp."

"Yes. They were in the sacred land."

"When did this get to be sacred land?"

"When the spirit told my brother. My brother would have killed them anyway, but they had to be killed specially to warn others away."

"And what did you have to do with this?" Ruff's eyes sharpened. He wasn't all that sure he wasn't being suckered in here. A beautiful young girl with a smooth line of patter, the cute trick of taking off her shirt and capturing a man's attention . . . she went on.

"The souls of the dead are damned. My brother rides the circle around them. Or when he cannot, he draws a circle near the dead. This keeps the white man from going to heaven and returning to the earth."

"You were riding some circles yourself."

She nodded emphatically. "Yes, in the opposite direction! This is so that the souls can go to heaven. That must be done. And I did as the priest showed me and made crosses of ash on their heads. That means they are Christians."

Ruff Justice just stared at her. Was this polymorphic religion of the woman's something real to her? Or was it something woven to please Ruff Justice and her idea of Christianity? Or a shadow of madness similar to her brother's? Justice had seen some odd permutations of religion among Indians when Christianity collided with native beliefs. You found it in Mexico, in Dakota, in California. The Spanish friars had had a way of adapting native rituals to their own purposes, of wedding Christianity to relics of barbarism.

She looked so sincere, so damned ingenuous that it was difficult to believe she was making all of this up. She had tried to do what was right, that was all.

Maybe.

"Get your shirt on," Ruff growled at her.

"It is not dry."

"Get it on anyway. I want you to help me do something," he said. "Something very difficult."

"I will help you if it does not kill."

"I can't even promise you that, but I don't *want* to kill to accomplish it."

She was pulling her shirt on and she talked through it. "What is it you would have me do?"

"I want you to draw the camp for me, to tell me what will happen tonight, how the ceremonies will go."

"No!" She snugged the shirt down and looked at him wide-eyed and fearful. She knew.

"Yes. That's what I want you to do."

"But—you mean to go into the camp."

Ruff meant to do just that. "Yes," he said, "that's what I'm going to do and I need your help."

"It is to die."

"Maybe. The other prisoners will die for certain if I don't try to get them out."

"Yes"—she waved a hand in a helpless gesture— "this is so—unless I can talk to my brother and tell him he must not kill people."

"You've told him that before."

"Yes."

"And it didn't do a damn bit of good, did it? Your brother likes to kill. He kills for the sense of power it gives him. I know this because of the way he kills.

Not in combat, not because a battle must be waged, but slyly, maliciously."

"I could tell him. . . ." Her head hung.

"You couldn't tell him anything he would listen to." Nor could Ruff do much in all probability, but there wasn't time to get help, there just wasn't. He was open to any alternative suggestion, but there were no bright ideas floating around on the breeze.

"If I go down there, then I can find out where they are," she said after a minute.

"And tell Eagle Spirit where I am."

"I would not do that!" she said, deeply offended—or apparently offended. Justice wasn't sure enough of what he had here to guess at her deeper motives. It could be she was a genuinely ingenuous, childlike thing, half educated and despising bloodshed. Or, and it was more likely all in all, she was a clever, clever woman.

"I can't chance it. You'll stay here, bound, when I go down into camp."

"You will tie me again!" Her eyes sparked as she considered that. "I do not like it."

"That's the way it's going to have to be." Ruff stood before her again, looking down at her pretty face, which slowly lifted to his. "Now, let's have a long conversation. I want to know where the captives will be, where the horses are, what the ceremony will consist of, where Eagle Spirit's tepee is."

"And how do you know I will tell you true?" the girl asked. "If you cannot trust me, how do you know?"

"I know because I am going down tonight, and if everything is not as you say it is, I am going to come back and cut off your ears and your nose."

"Ugh." She shuddered. "No nose. Like Mountain Bear's wife."

"No nose and no ears. Now. Will you tell me what I want to know?"

"I will tell you, but it is a mistake not to take me with you."

"Maybe so. I'll chance it. Take a stick and draw the camp in the dirt."

"What is your name?" she asked from out of the blue. She had picked up a stick and sat crouched against the dark earth beneath the tall oaks, looking up at him.

"Ruff Justice."

"Your people call you this?"

"Yes."

"Ruff Justice?" She smiled and cocked her head, writing it in the soil, spelling the first name "Rough."

Ruff toed out his name and squatted down. "Now, tell me how the land lies, where the creek is, where there is a tree. Everything."

"My name is Dawn Sky," the girl said, and her voice was softer than it had been, throaty, echoic.

"Yes."

"Will you say my name?"

"Dawn Sky," Justice said, and the girl smiled. Then she got to work, drawing the camp in detail down to the smallest point, and Justice crouched near her, hanging on every word, impressing it on his mind. It meant life or death to him, life or death to others. Norah Gates? Was she down there or was she in fact among the dead, or even hiding in the hills, frantic with fear? How about Ralston? If they had gotten him, it was no great loss, but there were others Ruff felt for. Reb Saunders and Johnny Albright, for instance. Sergeant Cornwall was almost certainly dead; Ruff had seen a man in uniform built too much like Cornwall to be anyone else. By now maybe the big sergeant was nothing more than an ivory skull on a wooden stake.

"No dogs?" Justice asked. "No dogs anywhere?"

"No. No dogs. Have I told you what you need to know, Ruff Justice?"

"I don't know." He looked into those dark, wide eyes, wanting to trust the innocence, the kindness he saw there, not quite able to do it. "I hope so, Dawn Sky."

"It is good."

"What is good?" Ruff, perplexed, asked.

"You have said my name again. I have become a person to you. If you name my name, then I have a soul."

"Sure." Ruff didn't want to spend time in the girl's metaphysical wonderland. She did have her ideas, that was sure. Odd ideas provided by a violent collision of conflicting cultures. Still, it didn't hurt to say her name and he spoke it again as he sat next to her, watching the sun ride higher into a cloudy morning sky.

"Dawn Sky."

And she rolled toward him, to lie, her eyes darkly luminous, lips slightly parted, looking up at him. Her lips moved and she silently formed two words.

"Ruff Justice."

Now what the hell can you make of that? Ruff asked himself. This wild thing whose half brother wanted to slaughter everything white, who wanted to make himself the big magic man for the entire Cheyenne nation, who ruled through slaughter and would likely on this night or another soon kill Ruff Justice—this wild thing would lie down with him. He looked into those dark eyes, wondering.

Perhaps she would cut off his head and ride triumphantly into Eagle Spirit's camp. When Bart had last seen her, she had been holding a dead man's head. According to Dawn Sky she had been trying to return it, to make sure that Tug Gates didn't lose his spirit. And if you believe everything you heard . . .

"Not now," he told her.

"Kiss me."

"Didn't I say not now?" he repeated roughly.

"Please."

And he gave in. There aren't many who wouldn't. He gave in and bent his face to hers, seeing the excitement in her eyes, hearing her rapid, shallow breathing. Her lips parted and he kissed her, an operation she seemed to know something about. Her lips were supple, warm. Her tongue brushed his lips lightly. Her arms were around him, drawing him to her, her hand resting on his waist.

"Uh-uh," he said, pulling back. That hand had gotten too close to his bowie knife.

"I am with you. I do not like the killing."

"So you told me."

Ruff got to his feet and picked up his torn blanket again.

"What are you doing?"

"I've got to sleep. I'm going to tie you up while I do."

"You will not sleep with me?"

"No."

"You do not trust Dawn Sky," she said with a childish whimper.

"No."

"I have told you I am a true woman."

"Move over next to that tree. We'll see if you are a true woman or not—tonight. If everything is not as you tell me, then I'll know you are not."

"But it will be. I could not lie to you."

"No, I know it," Ruff said, tying her to the tree,

hands behind the trunk. "No one can lie to me." But everyone kept on doing it.

Finished, he stood looking at her. Those eyes were still bright, but now they were a little accusing, hurt perhaps. She resented being tied, but that was just too bad. He had to watch out for his own neck.

"Good night," he said, and the eyes just stared at him as he walked away. Looking out across the broken hills, Ruff could see smoke rising through the drizzle of the day. Much smoke. Many fires. Many Cheyenne. It would be interesting.

He stretched out on his blanket, looked once more at the girl, who stared at him in stony silence, tipped his hat down over his eyes, and went to sleep.

"You are a crazy man, I think, Ruff Justice," the girl said, but there was no answer. She sighed, tested the bonds that held her hands, and frowned, settling back to watch the sleeping white man, the man who would make war on an entire tribe. "Crazy."

11.

The fires blazed hotly against the sky. A hundred ponies grazed in the darkness to Ruff Justice's left. Among the trees were more ponies and scattered tepees. The sound of the drums, repetitious, rhythmic, echoed through the cold and rainy night.

Ruff lifted his head another half an inch, his eyes searching the darkness with the intentness of a wild animal, a hunting thing. His hands were empty; the big Spencer rifle was of no use in a situation like this. He had left it in the cradling boughs of a big oak.

Justice had his look around. There were twenty or so tepees visible, more beyond the rise if Dawn Sky's word was good. There was an old ramshackle building not far away. That was the granary for the old French fort. The fort had been burned twenty years ago, but the granary, of native stone, still stood. And if they had thought to put their prisoners in there, getting them out was going to be a bitch.

"If any of them's alive."

Dawn Sky had thought her brother would keep them alive for display. To show the other Cheyenne leaders, some of whom were reluctant to flock to his banner. They would all be displayed and then the party would end with everyone merrily hacking the prisoners to death.

Justice pressed his head to the earth. A tall, lazily

walking shadow had appeared to his right. A briefly seen silhouette against the sky that showed between the black iron trunks of the big oaks.

The man spoke to someone out of sight. "The big tent . . . the magic tent . . ." Ruff couldn't get it. It was too fast for his trading-post Cheyenne.

Ruff's hand slipped behind his belt and withdrew the bowie knife from its sheath. If the Indian came any closer . . . but he didn't, not this time. Ruff relaxed slightly, surprised to find that tension had knotted that hand, cramped his biceps. You're getting old, my man, he thought mockingly. A few hundred butchers can scare you these days.

He waited until the night was silent and empty once again and then got slowly to his feet and moved on another hundred feet.

Pressing himself to the trunk of a huge, lightning-struck oak, he waited, his pulse hammering in his temples. The fires were nearer now, and he could see dancers moving around the weaving flames. Rain twisted down from out of an obsidian sky.

Somewhere ahead and beyond the fire lay Eagle Spirit's tent. It would be the largest of the tepees, the one with the magic symbols painted over it. Would the prisoners be there? Or in the "magic tent" the passing Cheyenne had mentioned. Perhaps they were one and the same.

Justice took a slow deep breath, chasing away the ranting demons that swarmed around him. Who was the more mad, Eagle Spirit or a lone white slipping into the camp of the Cheyenne?

It had happened.

Not for the first time, but for the first time in a long while. Ruff's blood had been racing, his eyes aching with tension, his muscles knotted, and then suddenly there was nothing. The anxiety had simply drained away, leaving him hollow, cold, emotionless.

It had happened before, many times, and it made him wonder if he *was* mad. It was his warrior's calm, his body's way of coping with stress. He had, before, waited among the dead and dying, a pistol in each hand, facing the charge of hundreds of Sioux warriors. Yes, he had even then felt fear, but it was a faraway emotion, something remembered and not felt. He had known simply that he was going to die—if not at that moment, then shortly, in an hour, a day, a year—and he was not going to go under as a coward. And so he had fought on, the wind blowing his long dark hair as he calmly emptied each pistol, firing with either hand.

Episodes like that had built his reputation. It meant nothing. It was a trick of the mind.

The calmness was there again now. He started forward, watching through the trees as the weirdly painted dancers continued to leap and spin, knees raised high, their naked bodies fire-glossed.

The Cheyenne sentry rose up from out of the shadows and his body collided with Ruff's.

Justice was knocked backward, his shoulder and head striking a tree as the exultant, silent young brave leaped at him and slashed at the long-haired white with his knife.

Ruff dove for the earth, saw the knife cut air before his face, strike the tree, and shatter, so brittle was the blade. He came to his feet and the Cheyenne came in again. In his hand was his battle-ax, a white-made steel ax with feathers tied to the handle below the head. Ruff backed away, his own bowie in his hand.

The Indian's eyes were brightened by the distant fires. He was flying high, was the Cheyenne. He had the white, had him dead to rights. A long-legged man with flowing hair, a white warrior who would die beneath his ax on this night. There would be a celebration for Fox Tree around the totem lodge. Fox Tree who had killed this white hunter.

Fox Tree was young and there was excitement coursing through his veins. He forgot all his father had taught him about the use of an ax, how the enemy should be whittled down, how the hands were the best targets, the hands, which could be severed without putting your own body within the reach of the opponent's knife blade. The hands, which could be crippled easily, through which the life's blood could flow as easily and as mortally as a heart wound.

Fox Tree leaped, grunting with effort and satisfaction. His ax rose high and he drove it down with all of his strength toward the white man's skull, wanting to cleave it, to split it wide and end the fight.

It was too fast, his movement too irrevocable, and Fox Tree knew as soon as he lunged that he had made a mistake, a fatal mistake.

The white hunter stepped inside of the blow and as Fox Tree's arm, the arm striking down with the ax, hit the white's shoulder, the knife blade was buried in Fox Tree's belly. Buried and twisted, the blade ripping up, the point touching heart muscle and lung while the Cheyenne tried frantically to pull away.

It was too late. The white man clung to him, not wanting to back away, not taking a chance that the ax might be wielded again with deadly results.

Fox Tree looked up into the rain and then slid slowly to the earth, the ax falling free. Ruff Justice turned, wiped back his long hair, and started jogging forward. His time had just been cut down. Eventually someone would find the dead brave. It might be some time in the darkness, in the rain; it might be momentarily. He had to take his best shot and get the hell out of there.

He slowed his pace and then halted, the breath steaming from his lips. The rain had increased, hammering down, muffling the sound of the drums, dulling the glow of the still-raging fires.

He was within sight of a large tepee. Around it, spiraling upward across the tanned buffalo hide, were the magic signs of the Eagle Spirit: many-armed suns, white buffalo, the secret eyes, the stars of the dark heaven.

It sat square in the middle of a clearing some hundred yards across. To reach it would be impossible. Ruff's heart sank. A hundred Cheyenne warriors stood around in the rain, blankets over their shoulders, some of them drinking what seemed to be corn liquor, others smoking pipes. There were oxen roasting over great pit fires. Oxen cut from the yokes of Stuyvestant's wagons.

Now the dancers were beginning to gather again. They wore strange costumes representing a pantheon of spirits. Ruff saw a bear mask, a dancer with a cougar's hide draped over him, his face painted red and yellow, his eyes ringed with black. Beyond him was a man painted white on one side of his body, black on the other. He wore nothing but a breechclout in the cold rain. Big magic was building.

Where was Eagle Spirit? And the captives. If they were still alive—that was an assumption of Dawn Sky's, that the prisoners were to be held and communally tortured on this rainy night.

Someone was coming.

Ruff moved swiftly to the other side of the tree where he stood crouched and ready. He had thought it was a man, but now he saw the antlers of a mule deer against the sky and frowned deeply until it became more obvious what he was looking at.

Another dancer, another medicine man, was hurrying toward the clearing. This one wore a deer's head, a rack of antlers on his head, a full suit of buckskin. Ruff made his decision instantly.

As the medicine man passed the oak he stepped out and clubbed him down. With a sigh the dancer sagged to the damp earth. Looking around, Ruff began stripping the dancer.

In another minute the deer dancer continued on. Inside the hide, hidden by the flap of skin that served as a mask, was the intruder, Ruff Justice.

"Come on, brother. Drink with us!" someone called out, and Ruff, not sure if they were speaking to him, waved a hand and hurried on. He didn't dare look back to see if anyone followed him.

He was among the tepees now, moving toward the large tent that belonged to Eagle Spirit. He passed three men walking together. One of them said something Ruff didn't get. He moved his hands in an indefinite, impatient gesture and hurried on.

How much time did he have? Five minutes? Less before the dead guard, the dancer, were discovered? He had made it this far only because the Cheyenne could not have expected a white to invade their camp. Not one man, not in the face of their numbers.

Once the dead man was discovered and the alarm raised, he wouldn't have a chance in hell.

He was beside the big tent now. All of thirty feet tall, it was painted over nearly every inch of hide. The vent above Ruff's head was open and smoke spiraled up into the cold night skies. Someone was within. Eagle Spirit? Ruff's heart gave a little leap. If he could be cut down now, there would be no uprising, there would be no more dead scattered about the plains.

Ruff stood in the deep shadows, looking through the rain, in one direction and then the other. There was no one around. Near the bonfires the dancing had

begun again, the tom-toms pounding away monot-
onously, ominously. And had they missed the deer
dancer yet?

Ruff took his bowie and slowly cut a three-inch-long
gash in the side of the tepee, near the pole. He leaned
his head to the slit and looked in. There was no one
there but an old man with many battle scars. He was
eating rapidly, wolfing down his food. There was no
sign of any prisoners, no sign of Eagle Spirit.

Where, then, were they being held?

"The old granary," Ruff told himself. It had to be.
He squatted there in the darkness, angry and dismayed.
That meant traveling all the way back across the
camp to where he had begun, risking detection with
each step.

And if he reached the granary? No telling. Too
many variables. Ruff started that way, keeping to the
shadows. His disguise had proven effective, but if someone who knew the deer dancer wanted to have a
conversation, it wouldn't work. Maybe the dancer was
supposed to be at the bonfire, likely he was. . . . Knock
it off, Justice! No sense worrying about it if you can't
help it, he told himself with some anger.

What could he help? He could plan ahead. How
many hostages? Uncertain. How many guards—again,
uncertain. They would need weapons once they got
out of the old stone building, and they would need
horses—that more than anything else.

Well, the Cheyenne were horse wealthy.

Justice walked through the oak grove, passing another silent warrior in full paint. He simply walked
up to where the horses were kept on a rope tied between two trees, untied them, and led the whole string
back through the shadowy night, expecting to feel
that arrow thud into his back at any moment.

But again he got away with his audacious plan.

Temporarily.

Again he passed Cheyenne warriors, two men sharing liquor from a bottle, blankets around them. They simply looked at him. Nothing was said and they passed in the night, Justice leading twenty horses.

He walked them away from the camp and left them in a dell where oak and cottonwood grew heavily together, where the foliage overhead was so thickly intertwined that it cut out the starlight and rain.

Then, circling up slope and through the heavy brush, panting as the surprisingly weighty costume dragged against his efforts, he worked his way toward the granary.

He lay for a long minute atop the ridge above the granary. Three guards he saw, and there might have been more. One of the Cheyenne seemed to have been talking to someone else in the trees.

"In there then," Justice said. He had struck it—they weren't guarding an empty stone building, that was certain.

The question was what to do about it, and something had to be done. It couldn't be long now before they came for the white captives. The celebration in the clearing beyond the screen of trees had reached a fever pitch. The dancing was wild, frantic, and threatening.

"Do it, Ruffin, do it or get the hell out," he told himself. Put like that there weren't many choices.

He started down the slope and toward the stone building. The guards watched him come. There was one at the door, or what had been the door to the decrepit building, one on the roof, one near the trees to Ruff's left. That was the nearest one, but Ruff chose to leave him until last. He would be screened out of the occurrences below if he stayed where he was. Justice lifted a hand and the Cheyenne waved back.

Inside the deerskin he wore Ruff held his knife in his right hand. The left hovered near the Colt, which was in his waistband now, handy. The pistol was a last resort. If he fired that pistol, he would be lighting the fuse to a powder keg. It had to be the knife, the knife that had already tasted blood on that night.

"You are late," the man at the door called to Ruff.

"I am sick," Ruff said, and he thought he saw the man stiffen. Suspicion? Or Ruff's imagination.

"Everyone is dancing. What are you doing here?"

"I am sick," Ruff said again, and then he half turned his back and leaned his hand against the wall as if bracing himself.

"What is it, too much whiskey?" the guard asked, walking to where Justice stood. "Eh? Too much liquor?"

Justice turned and sunk the bowie knife to the haft in the guard's belly, twisting, yanking, wanting it to be quick and silent. The guard's mouth opened and black blood spilled out. Ruff stepped back and the man fell to the earth. He rolled him into the shadows next to the stone building.

"What happened?"

The man on the roof had heard something. The body falling perhaps, the muffled groan that had escaped the dying man's lips.

Ruff's heart skipped a beat. He was holding the knife in his hand beside his leg. The dead man lay at his feet.

"What happened down there?" the Cheyenne demanded.

"Sick," Ruff said. "He is sick."

"Sick?" The Cheyenne's voice was cold and hard. He peered at Ruff, seeing only the deer mask, the antlers and hide. That and the crumpled shadow at his feet. "Well, what's the matter with him?"

"I don't know."

The Cheyenne leaped softly to the ground, walking to the body. "And what's the matter with you?" he asked Ruff. "What are you doing here? This is blood!"

Justice was behind the crouching man. The knife slashed a gaping mouth across his throat and the blood gurgled out. The second warrior pitched forward, strangling on his own blood, dying in moments as Ruff crouched, looking toward the woods and the last guard. There was no movement there, no sound of warning, yet how long could he go without being spotted, with the minutes piling up, with the dead strung out across the camp?

He moved swiftly to the door of the old granary and kicked it open.

Six people sat huddled in the darkness, their heads bowed, eyes looking up hopelessly as Ruff Justice in the deer dancer's suit filled the doorway to the old stone building.

"Get up," he said to them. "Get up and let's get moving."

12.

A quick look around the interior of the rat-infested old granary told Justice one thing. Norah Gates wasn't there. Silence was necessary, but at that moment so was knowing.

"Where's Norah Gates?" he asked the man nearest.

"You speak English?" the soldier asked the deer dancer.

"Damn you, it's Ruff Justice. Where's Norah Gates?"

"Mr. Justice! And who else would we expect, damn my eyes."

"Is that you, Reb?"

"It's me," the shadowy figure answered. "The woman wasn't with us. I don't know where she got to."

"Dead?"

"No. No, I don't think so."

"She was with Ralston," another soldier put in, "and the lieutenant made a getaway. I know," he added bitterly, "I saw him skedaddling when it started to get hot."

"All right. How about Stuyvestant?"

"With them."

"I'm not," a familiar voice said, and Ruff recognized Rudy Stuyvestant, big and hostile. "And where the hell were you, scout?"

"Cut off. I'll discuss it with you later if you need an explanation. Right now let's get before we turn into a collection of skinned heads. Now and quietly. I've got horses down in the trees. Reb, there's two Indians outside here who had weapons; you'd better snatch them up."

"All right."

"Easy now, boys. Softly. We might just make it out of this camp."

"Justice!" The voice was loud, overloud, the warning in its tone explicit. Ruff whirled to see the Cheyenne warrior in the doorway. The third guard who had grown impatient and suspicious. He had his gun in his hands, a grimace on his lips. And dark blood trickling from his mouth. The Cheyenne fell face forward into the granary.

The girl was behind him.

"Ruff Justice."

"Thought I left you somewhere else," Ruff growled. Dawn Sky just smiled. She had a hefty club in her hands. "And I thought you didn't believe in violence," he added.

"Not dead. Just a little sleep," she said, looking slightly regretful. "Come on, we must go."

She was right there. Reb hied past Ruff and got the rifles, keeping one himself, tossing one to Toby Ellis, a private soldier from Indiana. Ellis had a good shooting eye. The guns, however, weren't good for a hell of a lot. If the shooting started, Ruff reminded himself again, they would go down. Maybe it gave the men a comfort to hold them.

Rudy Stuyvestant brushed past Ruff and then two more private soldiers. The last man's eyes were ferret-bright, wild, watchful. Johnny Albright had his own concerns.

"Stick with us," Ruff told the kid.

"Sure." Albright grinned crookedly. Stick with the rest of them and let them hang him.

"They come," Dawn Sky said, tugging at Ruff's sleeve. Justice couldn't see or hear anyone coming, but he believed her. With a last glance back toward the war camp he started loping toward the hidden horses, Dawn Sky at his side.

He shed the costume in bits and pieces, and by the time they reached the ponies Ruff was in buckskins again. Reb Saunders had picked out a pony and was already up. Rudy Stuyvestant was slowly selecting one like a buyer at a horse auction.

"Get up and let's get," Ruff hissed.

The shot from behind them emphasized that idea. There was no doubt that the shot was a warning to the war camp, that the dead or the empty granary had been discovered. In a minute there was going to be a hundred or more warriors on their tails.

"Get," Ruff hissed again. "North and over the ridge."

"East." It was Dawn Sky who insisted. She took Ruff by the shoulder and half turned him. "There is a long canyon. They cannot follow us."

"Dawn Sky . . ."

Rudy Stuyvestant said too loudly, "Which is it? Do we listen to the squaw or not?"

"Mr. Justice? Someone's coming on the run."

He looked into her eyes, uncertain. "East," he said at last. "Take all the ponies we can. Herd 'em ahead of us. It'll confuse things." Then he was up and aboard a spotted pony, one of many that still wore a hackamore. Beside him was Dawn Sky. Ruff heeled his pony forward sharply, through the trees, hazing the string of horses before him. There was another shot from behind, much nearer now, but they were mounted and running, riding through the dark and rain. Eastward.

They came out of the trees and onto open grassland. The rain, which had been falling fitfully, had stopped again and by the starlight they could see the country around them gradually rising, building toward the bluffs ahead.

Ruff looked back across his shoulder. He couldn't see them, but they were there. Everyone knew it, felt it. The idea of outfighting the Cheyenne was simply ridiculous. They had to run and run far.

They were heading east now, but to Ruff's mind their destination had to be Morgan Creek to the west. Fort Lincoln was days away across open prairie.

"Here they come," Reb shouted. There was no need for silence now.

Here they came all right, and it sent a chill through Justice. Across his shoulder he could see a dozen, two dozen, tiny figures on horseback. A loud, trilling cry echoed across the flats as the lead warriors spotted the fleeing soldiers.

On the heels of the cry a volley of shots was fired and one of the soldiers in front of Justice, tagged by a luckless bullet, went down to be trampled over by the horses behind.

"The canyon?" Ruff shouted at Dawn Sky.

"It is there."

"Where, dammit!"

He could see nothing but the black wall of a bluff rising off the plains, nothing to indicate a canyon mouth. Was it there? Was Dawn Sky playing some strange game of her own? It had to be the truth, had to—he had thrown caution to the winds and accepted her word. If that had been a mistake, it was a fatal one. Every one of them would die.

"There," she said again, and Ruff saw a star shining in a notch in the bluff, a glittering, steel-blue promise. "Just ahead."

Ruff urged the little spotted pony onward. Another volley of shots was fired from behind, but there were no hits. Jolting across the prairie on horseback, in the dark, it would have been surprising if anyone had been hit. But then one man had already proven that the odds weren't always with you.

"There it is! Reb! Right there."

"I see it, Mr. Justice."

"It could be a box canyon," Rudy Stuyvestant shouted. "Get on in there."

"It's a trap!" Stuyvestant's horse turned in a frantic circle. The Cheyenne, whooping and shooting, were closing the distance now.

"Then stay out here and take your chances," Ruff snapped angrily. He kneed his pony and rode on, still leading a short string of extra horses.

In the canyon darkness, coolness closed around them. Ruff wondered if there was any chance Stuyvestant was right. Could it be a box canyon? That was the most usual formation in this kind of country. Two shifting faults slid in opposite directions and you had a box canyon, useful for cattlemen as natural corrals, deadly for the hunted.

He looked at Dawn Sky as they rode the sharply uptilting trail toward the notch above.

"There is a way. Do not look so evil."

He looked evil, did he? Well, he felt evil just now. Damned evil. He looked above him, searching for and finding a shelf of rock that looked unsteady enough— but there was no way up there.

The Indians had entered the canyon. Behind them a series of war whoops, little doglike yips, filled the air. They all rode a little more swiftly. The trail was becoming narrow, the drop-off on the north side perilous. The bluff rose steeply to their right, shouldering against them, squeezing them toward the drop-off.

"All right, it's going to be too narrow in a minute," Ruff Justice said, pulling up his lathered pony.

"What are you talking about?" Rudy Stuyvestant

screeched. "What are you doing? They're riding in our tracks, Justice."

"I know where they are, damn you." Ruff had reached the limit of his patience with the big blond kid.

"Now, Mr. Justice?" Reb Saunders asked. Reb was quick; he knew what was up.

"No, let them get a little higher. Into the narrow bend."

"What is this?" Johnny Albright asked calmly, as if he didn't have a care in the world. Maybe he had been on the ragged edge for so long that his nerves had simply frozen, just as Justice's had at this moment. Albright sat there quietly, listening to the war whoops, seeing the shadowy insect-sized figures riding the steep trail.

"We're going to give them a little welcome, Johnny. Haze those spare ponies up here. Keep them together, keep them pointed downhill."

"Yeah." There was a touch of glee in Albright's voice. He and Toby Ellis pushed their little string forward, cutting the lead rope from the hackamores so that each horse was free of the other.

The Cheyenne were gone now, out of sight as they rounded a sharp bend in the trail. A moment later they reappeared, startlingly near, their guns held high, their war cries loud and savage.

"Do it!" Ruff Justice yelled, and the men behind him fired their guns into the mob of approaching Cheyenne. They didn't hit much, but the gunfire was enough to spook the Indian ponies in front of them. They broke into a wild-eyed run, stampeding down the narrow mountain trail. Ruff fired his six-gun into the air as he fought to hold back the spotted pony he rode with his other hand.

The shouts of warning from below were too late. The Cheyenne couldn't turn their horses on the narrow trail and there was no place to go. They could only sit and suffer the brunt of the stampede. Horse collided with horse, ponies rearing into the air, throwing their riders. Ruff saw one and then another man and horse shouldered off the rim of the trail, the men screaming, the horses whickering as they fell toward the rocks below.

"Let's go," Ruff said. And he turned his horse.

Still the trail climbed, and still the Cheyenne would be pursuing. They wouldn't quit; they would only grow more resolute as they suffered casualties. And Justice knew they couldn't inflict enough casualties to matter. If fifty were killed, that left another fifty, three hundred more back in the war camp. An unstoppable force for his pitiful handful.

"Ride on," he shouted to Reb, drawing his horse up.

"What's up, Mr. Justice?"

"Just ride on, Reb. I'll be along."

He gave Saunders the reins to his horse. The soldier took them obediently, but he obviously didn't know what was going on. Nor did Dawn Sky, who started to demand, "What are you doing? Do not leave me."

"How much of this trail left?" Ruff asked, ignoring her questions.

"A little way. Half a mile. Then there is flat meadow. some trees."

"All right. I'll be there soon."

"Justice . . ."

He leaned forward and kissed her briefly. Then he stood on the back of the horse and leaped up, grabbing hold of the gnarled roots of a manzanita. He got a toehold and then another grip on a higher, more firmly rooted bush, and then was off the trail, standing on a ledge above it.

He waved his arm furiously. The party of soldiers hadn't yet started on up the trail. Perhaps they thought he was doing some sort of circus act for their entertainment.

"Go," Ruff said soundlessly. Then he turned to his work; they would have to do their part on their own. He worked his way back along the rocky ledge. The earth beneath him was soft from the recent rain. All around towers and walls of ancient stone stood crumbling.

He had spotted this chance from the trail below. And now, while the Cheyenne were still disorganized, was the time to do it. If he could.

Ruff shoved a few loose rocks onto the trail below, testing. Then he moved to the larger stacks of decaying granite, putting his back to it. He squatted down, bending his legs, then straightening them, arms braced, muscles taut with the exertion. Nothing happened and he swore softly. The stack of rocks looked rotten enough to fall apart in a strong wind, but it didn't want to budge for him.

"Again," Justice encouraged himself. He could hear the sounds of approaching horses now and adrenaline surged through his body. He strained against the rocks—did something give?—until the sweat was pouring out of him despite the coldness of the night.

"Terrific idea, Justice," he muttered. And he had sent the others blithely forward, trusting to the magnificent leadership of the redoubtable plainsman. Who was now executing his shrewd plan by leaning with all his strength against a pile of immovable boulders.

He laughed. Ruff laughed, choking on it. He again tried to dislodge the rocks, his thoughts bitter and . . . evil. The horses were closer now, the war whoops shrill and clear. Something moved. Something in that vast, unsteady pyramid of rock shifted and gave, sagged forward.

But it would not fall!

Justice hurled himself against the rocks, kicking one small boulder onto the trail in sheer desperation. He could see the Indians rounding the bend, not more than fifty yards off. Again he put his back to the stones, his teeth clamped together, the tendons of his body standing taut, his lean muscles and ligaments popping with the strain.

It gave. It went in a thundering roll, a night-shattering rumble, the bank below the rocks giving way as the tower of stone buckled and fell, boulders bounding off into space, the bluff sloughing onto the trail below. A Cheyenne screamed, and a horse was broken by tons of falling rock.

Justice watched it for a moment, watched the clouds of falling earth, the stone and mud that shut off the trail. Then he turned and started up slope.

He climbed over the broken ground and then dropped to the trail again to jog on as the thin starlight began to fade and the rain again began to fall.

He ran on knowing that they hadn't gained a damn thing. They had held the Cheyenne back for an hour, a night, but there was no way off the plains with the Indians on their heels. Not tonight, but tomorrow, and if not then, then the day after for certain. The Cheyenne would run them to the ground.

They were waiting for him in the shadows of the cedar trees. Wind-twisted, gnarled little trees, they would endure longer than the men who strutted across the earth proclaiming themselves masters of nature.

"Ruff Justice!" Her exclamation was breathy. Her arms around his neck and she clung to him tightly.

"Howdy, woman," he said, managing a grin. He was beginning to respect the woman very much. That wasn't to say he understood the workings of her mind—that was probably unfathomable.

"Did you kill them all?"

"She do have faith in you, don't she?" Reb Saunders cracked.

"She does—apparently." Ruff wiped his sleeve across his forehead. The sweat still beaded his skin. "No, I didn't kill them all. I'm not sure I killed any of them," he told the gathered men, "but I managed to close the trail off. They can't ride their horses up over the bluff, so they'll either have to continue on foot—which doesn't seem real likely—or circle around the bluff and wait for us to come down. That will take them some time. Either way, we'd better get moving again and keep moving until we can't move anymore."

"My horse pulled up lame," Toby Ellis said.

"All right. Ride up with me."

"My horse has some size," the other private soldier said. "More than yours, Mr. Justice."

"All right. You take him and then I'll relieve you. We'll switch around."

"Which direction, Mr. Justice?" Reb Saunders asked.

That was a good question. If anyone knew the answer, it was Dawn Sky. Ruff looked a query at her.

"North. There is no way down there."

"That makes sense," Rudy Stuyvestant grumbled.

"No good way. Just a bad way. They will not think we dare it," the Cheyenne girl said.

"All right," Justice decided quickly. "That's it. Across the bluff to the north. If we make it down on the flats, we try for Morgan Creek. We try real sudden."

"Why not Lincoln?"

"Too far."

"There can't be more than a hundred people in Morgan Creek; we'll be leading the Indians to them."

"They'll get hit anyway. This way they'll at least have some warning," Justice said, tired of explaining his thinking to them. Every once in a while he almost wished he had a bit of tin on his shoulders. The men would follow a fool into hell if he had enough brass on his body.

"Stuyvestant?"

"What is it?" Rudy was still surly, still carrying that grudge apparently.

"Did you see your father get away from the gold camp?" Justice asked as they started their horses northward, riding silently across the headland of the cedar-stippled bluff. The rain was misting down again.

"I saw him. He and Ralston. They had the girl—and the gold," Rudy said with some bitterness. Why wouldn't he be bitter? His father had pulled out with the gold dust, leaving him to make do as best he could.

"She was all right? Norah Gates was all right?"

"She was alive," Rudy said sullenly. "And that's more than we're likely to be soon, isn't it?"

He deliberately turned his horse away from Justice then and rode alone on the fringe of the party, a young man prematurely disappointed with life.

The hours passed, taut and dark and shivering, and they reached the northern end of the bluffs to stand looking down at a dark prairie, like an endless sea rolling away.

"Jesus," Reb Saunders said in a whisper. "We going down there?"

It didn't look possible. The bluff simply broke off and left a sheer cliff face standing. It was two thousand feet down and Ruff couldn't see a goat track along the cliff. He looked to Dawn Sky, who shrugged.

"It is hard. Not tonight. It can't be done at night, not by your people."

"We can make it in the daytime?" Ruff asked uncertainly.

Dawn Sky shrugged. "It has been done. They will not expect us here."

"All right." Ruff turned back to Reb. "We've come this far trusting the lady. We might as well go along with her now. We've an hour or two before light. Why don't we roll up and get some sleep."

"I'm willing to try," Reb said. He glanced to the rainy skies and shook his head. The night was cold, the ground was hard, and they had nothing for warmth but the horse-smelling Indian blankets. Yet they all needed rest badly. They had been going on adrenaline, on fear-sharpened nerves. You could only go on so long that way. Morning, on that cliff, would be no time to lose concentration to exhaustion.

"Do your best. It looks like we can find some shelter back in the cedars."

"Sentries out, Mr. Justice?" Toby Ellis asked.

"Doesn't seem much point in it, Toby."

"No, I don't reckon there does. I just wanted to ask. 'Night, Mr. Justice. I don't know about the rest of you, but I can sleep all right. I'm ready to drop now."

He went off into the trees with Reb, Rudy Stuyvesant, and the other two. Johnny Albright went last, looking up into the rain, his face strangely expressionless. The kid had lost it sometime back.

"You too?" Dawn Sky asked.

"What?"

"You will sleep too, Ruff Justice."

"Yes, after I see to the horses. There's some grass down below where we can picket them."

"Yes. I will help you."

"All right," Ruff agreed. "Unless you want to turn in too. You've had a rough day and night."

"I will help you . . ." She hesitated. "Ruff, have I proven I am a true woman?"

Justice, leading the horses, stopped to look down at her. "Yes, Dawn Sky, you have proven that."

"Then you will sleep with me now?" she asked.

And he told her, "Yes. Now I will sleep with you."

Together they led the horses to the patch of grass between the big rocks farther down the slope and then, while the night drifted over, they made their bed together.

13.

They went to a cleft in the rocks. There the wind was cut by the big boulders and the ground beneath them was halfway dry. With the blankets from the ponies they made their bed.

Justice undressed and lay down first. He watched Dawn Sky as she tugged her wet shirt up over her head. In the darkness she was a beautiful, tantalizing silhouette, catlike, lithe. She was out of her skirt and boots a moment later and she came to him shivering as he held the blanket up for her and then wrapped it around her, closing her in as she snuggled close to him and their bodies warmed one another.

For a while they did not move. The night was cold and only slowly did their bodies heat. Dawn Sky clung to him, her breath soft and warm against his throat, her breasts pressed against his chest.

Her thighs, long and smooth, were pressed against Ruff's and now her hand, which had been warming between her own legs, reached out tentatively and encircled his growing erection. He heard her suck in her breath sharply with pleasure, felt her shift, and lift her leg to throw it over his hip as she scooted nearer in the darkness, her lips moving across his shoulder and throat to his mouth.

"You are cold, I will keep you warm," she whispered.

"You are warm."

"Warmer there, yes? Inside I am warm. Very warm; I am built that way for you, to take you in and sleep you through the night."

And she did. She moved her hips again and Ruff slid easily inside her. Dawn Sky's head lolled on her neck, her eyes bright in the darkness, her hands eagerly helping him to enter her, to fill her.

His own lips dropped to her breasts and brushed against her dark, taut nipples as his hands slid down her hips and cupped her solid buttocks, drawing her nearer, feeling the clutching of her hands, the cushioned thrust of her pelvis, the ripe firmness of her breasts, the eager searching of her lips, the sudden wetness within Dawn Sky.

She began to tremble and then to writhe, to claw at him as she spread her legs wider, her body lush and eager as Ruff Justice rolled onto his back. She followed him anxiously, straddling him, her hands braced against his shoulders as her back arched; her head was thrown back, her long dark hair falling free to her breasts. Breasts that swayed from side to side, softly pendulous as Ruff's hands and lips teased them.

He could see her against the stars and clouds of the night sky, see her teeth bared with concentration, feel the slow settling of her body, the soft grinding of her pelvis and buttocks against him, the wetness of her seeping onto his thighs as she moved more eagerly, deliberately increasing her cadence, holding herself back with the greatest of efforts.

Justice reached up suddenly and gripped her hair at the nape of her neck. He pulled her face to his roughly and kissed her until her lips burned, until they were nerveless, bruised, as he arched his body and hammered against her. Dawn Sky twisted and moaned, her fingers clawing at his shoulders as his hard, demanding body probed hers, lifted her higher, drove her toward a completion that rushed upon her almost like a feared, dominating thing, overpowering her despite her feeble resistance, thundering across her body and sending her spinning as her body drained itself, flowered, grew sweet and heavy, its ripeness bursting over Ruff Justice, warming him as he found his own urgent climax and stiffened, clasping her to him as the cold night swept past.

They lay together without speaking, without moving except for the simple act of drawing the blankets up over them. The cold night had become warm and full, soft and rich. Neither of them slept or tried to. Tomorrow they might die. Tonight they wanted the sensation of being alive, the close touch of another human being.

She was, Ruff Justice decided, a true woman. A truer woman had never walked the plains. He still did not understand her; and he had about given that up. She with her bogies and spirits and bits and pieces of religion, shards of culture. She who walked with a brother she hated, who had been raised by a holy man who must have been something of a sensualist, she who had the fate of every man there in her hands, who now touched and held the essence of this one man, the warm earthy essence of Ruff Justice.

Dawn was a dull red flush along the eastern horizon, the slow, heavy stretching of stiff, cold muscles. Dressing in the near-darkness, shivering, breathing out clouds of steam, watching the naked woman dress: an incredible, primitive sight.

Then there were the horses, slick with frost that had to be rubbed from their backs; the men above standing in a huddled circle, speaking quietly, watching Ruff and the woman stride up the hill, seeing the suspicion and dull anger in some of the eyes, the hopeful expectation in others.

"I was over looking down that bluff this morning," Toby Ellis said, "and if there's a way down, it's so punk that my eyes can't find it. I didn't see a thing a horse could hope to manage."

"It's sheer cliff face, Mr. Justice," Reb commented,

"The girl says there's a way," Ruff replied.

"She might say it, but that don't make it so."

"There's no point in worrying about it now. That's the way we're going. Unless you want to go back."

They looked to the south where the Cheyenne camp was. No one spoke in favor of returning.

"All right then," Ruff said a little sharply. "It's on ahead. We'll give it a try."

Dawn Sky led them to the rim where the wind gusted coldly off the plains. Gray thunderheads in neat procession were stacked against the skies. The woman cast back and forth along the rim.

"It has been a long while—since I was a child," she explained.

Rudy exploded, "Damn her, there probably isn't even a way! Since she was a kid? You know how a kid's memory is, Justice."

"It's a little different with an Indian kid. They remember what they're shown. It may be important to their survival. The elders impress it on their minds."

Rudy Stuyvestant snorted derisively. The others just looked stranded helplessly between faint hope and despair.

"Here it is," Dawn Sky said finally, and they rushed to her. They stood looking down at an eyebrow of a trail that snaked down the cliff at an impossible angle. It seemed a hand's breadth wide, crumbling, slick. Ruff thought a horse, a good one, could negotiate it as far as he could see, but what happened beyond that? The trail snaked into a deep cut and then was lost. Time changes everything and it could be the trail was washed out farther down, vanished. There would be no hope at all of turning around down there, not with the horses. The best they could do if that happened would be to abandon the animals and come back up onto the plateau—to face the Cheyenne who would surely have found them by then.

"Well, Mr. Justice?" Reb asked.

"Those that can't fly are going to have to try it," Ruff said soberly.

"I'm scared of heights, scared stiff!" This was the fourth enlisted man, the one named Dryer. He was young, redheaded, freckled, silent. He was trembling now. A part of that might have been the cold, but a deal of it was plain fear.

"I'm scared of them too," Ruff said. "Anyone with good sense is. That's not the point. We've got to go down or die."

"I can't."

"You can," Justice said sharply. "I'm not leaving you here. You get on that horse of yours and come ahead. If you want to close your eyes, you do that. You can't help the horse much anyway. I'll lead you if you want, but dammit, don't give in to the fear, boy. If you do, you're dead, and you're liable to take someone with you."

"The soldier's got a right to be scared," Rudy Stuyvestant said. "Look at that. Feel that wind too. It'll blow a man right off that bootlace of a trail."

"I take it you're staying behind," Ruff said. He was a little sour on Rudy Stuyvestant, had been for a good long time.

"Not me. I want to see the end of this. I want to see what happens when we do get down to the flats. Hell, Justice, you might as well have left us in the war camp. At least it would be over by now."

"Maybe," Ruff said. "But the Indians have a way of

making death last when they want to. If I were you, I wouldn't be wishing for anything like that: it just might come true."

"Ruff Justice."

"Yes, Dawn Sky."

"I think they come." She was looking to the south, toward the cedar forest. Again Ruff could see nothing—and his eyes were generally accepted to be better than the average man's when it came to spotting movement—but he believed the woman. They would be coming. Eagle Spirit would not let the whites get away. It just might puncture a hole in his magic to do so.

"He will beat me," Dawn Sky said. "If he catches us, he will beat me badly." She looked to Ruff and said, "I have not told you the whole truth. He is not my brother."

"No?"

"He stole me. From the reservation. Eagle Spirit is my husband. He forced me to marry him, Ruff Justice."

"Christ," Reb Saunders muttered. "Now you know he won't give it up! How can he? He'd lose face, wouldn't he? A white man stealing his squaw from him."

"I am sorry, Ruff Justice. I was afraid to tell you before. I feared you would not think me a true woman."

"All right. It doesn't matter. They're coming anyway. The important thing is to get moving. Dammit, men, get up on those ponies! We're going down."

Down that road to hell. One way or the other. Ruff looked into the dizzying depths and felt a little of the fear that had turned Dryer's face gray and stiff.

"Dawn Sky?"

"I will go first," she said. Ruff Justice kissed her.

"I hope your magic is good," he said.

"My magic is the Lord, Ruff Justice," she reminded him.

"All right. Then we're going to be safe."

"Yes." She nodded with certainty. "We will be safe."

Ruff didn't share her certainty, but there wasn't any other choice, and their time was gone. Now he too could see, distantly, shadows moving through the forest, a flash of color against the green and red-brown of the cedars.

Dawn Sky started her pony, the animal shying, fighting the hackamore as the rocks crumbled underfoot. She forced the animal over, and in a moment there was nothing to be seen of her. Ruff looked at the others.

"I'll go last," he told them.

Reb Saunders took in a breath and blew it out sharply. "I'm next, I reckon."

He urged his horse forward and it dropped over the rim, out of sight. Rudy Stuyvestant, stiff and pale, followed. Then Toby Ellis, his teeth clenched.

The redhead held back. He was ashen, trembling.

"Let's have at it, Dryer."

"I can't, Mr. Justice, I just can't."

"Then give me your gun, damn you."

"My gun?" Dryer asked blankly.

"I'll put a round through your brain for you so you won't have to take what the Cheyenne have got in mind."

"You . . . Mr. Justice, you're kidding."

"Not at all. You've chosen death instead of a chance at life. All right; I'll make your death an easy one. You've seen tortured men before. You were with us at Ash Fork, weren't you? Don't you recall how they had staked Nate Calahan down and opened his belly, how they'd heaped burning tinder on his guts? How they'd tied his kid down faceup to the sun and cut his eyelids off so that the sun'd burn holes in his eyes. . . ?"

Dryer had his own eyes closed tightly. "That's enough," he said.

"Then you want me to kill you?"

"I want to give it a try. Damn you, Mr. Justice, I want to do anything I have to do to stay alive."

"Then let's have at it," Justice said, and he said it brusquely. No sense in letting the kid know now that Ruff could never have done what he threatened to do.

Dryer started his horse over the edge of the rim, his eyes wide, every muscle in his body locked with fear. Dust and rock fell away from the trail and for a moment Justice thought he had done it—killed the man in the way he feared—but the horse found its footing and, being a herding animal, proceeded down the trail, following the others of its kind.

With a last glance back, Ruff Justice started after the others.

His spotted pony had proven itself to be game and agile, but even so it was wary of this trail. It had every right to be. Justice's right leg brushed the rising face of stone on the horse's right flank. His right boot was dangling over space, the drop four hundred feet or so to a ledge, another four or five hundred to the dark plains.

The wind was gusting, pressing them against the bluff, at times picking up handfuls of sand and hurling them with seeming maliciousness into their eyes.

Ruff couldn't see Dawn Sky any longer; she had apparently rounded an unseen bend in the trail. Yes, that was it, for now Reb also vanished from view. It was an eerie sight, as if the mountain were swallowing the riders. They were there and then they were gone, disappearing into what appeared to be solid stone.

Dryer was tense and rigid with fear. He gripped the reins as if he would squeeze moisture from them. His eyes were straight ahead always, looking into the distances. He too rounded the bend and then it was Ruff's turn.

He found them all together, halted, their faces scored with lines of fear. The trail was gone.

"Look at this, Justice. This is what you've done!"

"Shut up, Stuyvestant."

Ruff stepped down from his horse and went forward, squeezing between the horses and the rising bluffs. He found Dawn Sky hunched beside the horse she rode, looking at the broken trail.

"Storms and time have devoured it," she said.

And they had. There was a stretch some fifteen to twenty feet wide where the trail had crumbled away, leaving a treacherous gap.

"Well?" Reb Saunders asked. "We go back?"

"No. There's no going back, Reb."

"How then?"

"We might make it over."

"You're not kidding?" Reb eyed the trail and shook his head. "No horse is going to make that leap."

"No," Ruff agreed. "We're going to have to leave them."

"I'm not sure a man can make this jump, Ruff."

"Neither am I, Reb," Justice said with a smile.

It wasn't the distance but the narrowness of the trail that confounded them. With a downhill start they should be able to clear the fifteen feet or so they had to jump, but they would then have to land on a ribbon of trail two to three feet wide. To land and hold steady. If they lost their balance, they would fall hundreds of feet.

"What does he want to do?" Rudy asked. The blond man was highly agitated now. "Jump that? We'll never make it."

"We'll make it or give ourselves up to the Cheyenne. What's the choice there?"

"The horses . . . what'll we do on the flats without horses?" Stuyvestant demanded.

"Try for it." Ruff shrugged. He didn't have a good answer. Yes, they needed the horses, but they were of no use if they couldn't leap that chasm and land on the trail. And they couldn't. They were Indian ponies, not mountain sheep.

Everyone understood that, although there was a lot of grumbling, mostly on Stuyvestant's part. Everyone knew there was only one way down now.

"Who's first?" Reb Saunders asked slowly.

"Me," Justice said.

"Let me go first, Ruff Justice," Dawn Sky said. The wind was gusting up the canyons, twisting her dark hair, fluttering the buckskin fringes on her shirt. "I can jump. I am a good jumper."

"I'm going first. I want you to come after me. I want to catch you if there's any trouble."

"And who will catch you, Ruff Justice?"

He squeezed her shoulder and smiled. "I won't miss."

And that was easier said than done. Ruff looked again at the break in the trail. The wind was twisting and thrusting against him. Well, when it has to be, it has to be. There wasn't a lot of point in thinking about it.

Ruff Justice backed up the trail some twenty feet, forcing the onlookers and their horses back. He winked then at Dawn Sky and took off.

His long legs stretched out and gathered speed. The chasm was suddenly upon him, appearing deeper, wider than ever. The wind buffeted him as he left the ground, arms churning. He had a moment as he hung in space four hundred feet above the earth below to consider a career change. Then he hit the trail on the far side of the gap, his legs jackknifing up. He felt his boot go briefly over the edge of the crumbling ledge, and he threw himself flat to keep from rolling.

Then he turned, sat up, and sat grinning back at his companions. "Well?"

"You made it by a good five feet, Mr. Justice," Reb yelled.

"Dawn Sky—you're next."

"I . . . I can do it," she said. There was a noteworthy lack of confidence in her words. She backed up the trail as Justice sat crouched and braced at the edge of the gap, waiting to help her if she needed help. Dawn Sky hoisted her skirt and tucked it into the waistband. Then she was off and flying, her hair twisting in the wind, streaming out behind her.

Her eyes met Ruff's even as she leaped. There was something besides fear in them—supplication, perhaps. Ruff backed away as it was obvious she was going to make it, if not by much. She hit the edge of the trail and pitched forward, Ruff reaching out to grab her by the waist and spin her to him.

"I do not do that again," she said with a gasp.

"Let's hope not," Justice answered with a a tight little smile. "Okay, Reb."

"Get out the net," Saunders cracked. There was a tenseness behind the joke, however. He too backed up, got a running start, and hurled himself frantically through space. He made it with plenty to spare. "I was scared enough to jump fifty feet," he said. "Damn." He leaned back against the wall of the bluff and put a hand to his heart, shaking his head.

Johnny Albright was next. There was no conversation before or after his jump. He simply did it, looked all of them in the eye, and sat down on the trail, staring into space. Toby Ellis made it easily, but started to go over the rim as a nasty gust of wind caught him landing. Ruff and Reb grabbed an arm each and dragged him back. Toby was shaking a little and no one blamed him for it.

"All right, Dryer!" Ruff called. There was only Dryer and Rudy left on the far side. The kid shook his head decisively.

"No."

"No, hell, let's go!"

"No." There was no emphasis, only cold determination. He was not going to jump.

"Then get the hell out of the way," Rudy Stuyvestant said. "I'll go. I'm not waiting here for the Cheyenne."

Reb Saunders yelled out, "Dryer, I'm ordering you to jump." The kid just looked at him. He shook his head negatively.

It was Johnny Albright who turned the trick. "Scared to die?" he taunted. "Hell, I was too. But I figure I'm already dead, just living on grace. You too, Dryer. Hell, man, you're dead! The Cheyenne got you, got all of us. What does it matter if you fall? You tell me what's the difference, really?"

"For God's sake, Albright . . ." Ellis began, but Johnny silenced him with a sharp gesture.

"Shut up. He knows what I mean—don't you, Dryer? Walking around dead like you are and you're scared to make a lousy jump. Well, jump off, then, you're holding us up!"

It worked. Why, how, Ruff didn't know, but it worked. Something inside Dryer was stung, his pride piqued, maybe. He backed up half a dozen steps, his fists clenched, his face red with rage or determination. Then with an explosive yell he raced down the trail and leaped.

They caught him and hauled him aboard.

"Okay, Rudy."

Stuyvestant was the heaviest of them all and that

caused Justice to move nearer the gap. Big men aren't great leapers; Stuyvestant wouldn't be any exception. He loped down the trail like an ox on the loose, launched himself into space, his hands windmilling.

"He's short!" someone yelled.

"Catch him!"

Ruff was the only one in position to try catching him. There was only room for one man there. Stuyvestant's eyes went wide as he saw he wasn't going to make it. He clawed at empty space, trying for a handhold on the wind. Then he hit the edge of the trail, his toes striking briefly as he fell back and down. His mouth opened and a scream of terror poured out.

The big hands flailed and Ruff Justice grabbed one as the man fell past. Stuyvestant came up with a jerk, nearly ripping Ruff's arm from its socket. And then he was holding Stuyvestant in space, the dangling man's life depending on the grip of Ruff Justice's left hand—and that grip was going as gravity tugged at Rudy Stuyvestant and Justice began to lose the uneven contest.

He could feel his own body being dragged toward the rim, and looking down, he could see Stuyvestant's pleading eyes. Then someone grabbed Ruff's feet and put the brakes on. Rudy found a small toehold and lifted himself up a little while Ruff got a new grip and pulled him up and over, and the two men sat side by side on the trail, feet dangling into space, panting deeply.

"Why?" Rudy asked.

"Why what?"

"Why did you . . . pull me up? Almost got yourself killed."

"It's what you needed . . . I don't hold a grudge, Rudy. Not over what's . . . passed between us." Great gasping breaths interrupted Ruff's words, but he was

steadying now, and he got slowly to his feet, wiping
back his long dark hair as he looked out across the far
plains below.

"I've been a real pain in the ass, I guess," Rudy
Stuyvestant said.

Ruff Justice looked down at the blond kid. "Yes,
that's right. You have been." Then he grinned, gave
Rudy his hand, and helped him to his feet, "Let's get
moving," he said, turning to the others. "The Cheyenne will be coming."

"Going?" Dryer said quietly, looking down the long
trail to the empty land beyond. "Where are we going
anyway? Albright was right, you know. He was right:
we're already dead men. Not just him and me, but all
of you. We're all dead, we're only looking for a place to
be buried."

14.

The wilderness trail meandered down the slope of the bluff. They were deep in shadow at moments and at other times in clear sunlight. They were visible for a long way if anyone happened to be out there watching. They had gambled that no one would be; if they had placed their chips on the wrong number, then they would die before sunset.

The trail began to widen and flatten, and here and there cottonwoods and sycamores grew. They had entered a long canyon where the shadows lay deep. The air was heavy with the scent of sage.

They paused in the coolness to catch their breath and to relieve the tension of their muscles, knotted with anxiety.

"Nice spot," Reb Saunders said, looking around. "Quiet—be nice for a picnic if a man had himself a lady."

"Nice spot," Ruff Justice agreed.

"West you figure, Mr. Justice? West toward Morgan Creek?"

"I think we'll have to do it that way."

"I guess Lincoln's too damned far. I don't suppose the colonel's going to ride up and find us here, is he?" Reb smiled faintly. He patted at his forehead with a big red handkerchief.

"I don't suppose so."

"Mr. Justice—reckon we'll make it?"

"Sure," Ruff said, but he wasn't even convinced himself. It seemed flatly impossible. They were thirty miles from Morgan Creek and the country was flat and open. There were four hundred Cheyenne back there looking for them, including one angry medicine man who wanted his bride. "Sure, we'll make it. Why not?"

When Reb was gone, Dawn Sky said, "If I go back, perhaps he will give this up."

"You know that's not true."

"I could talk to him."

"If he gave you the chance."

"He would not hurt me," Dawn Sky said. She crouched beside Ruff, touching his hair, her eyes intent and searching.

"You stay with us," Ruff growled. "I mean it."

"Yes, Ruff Justice!" She smiled brightly and rose, her eyes shining. "If you tell me to stay with you, I will."

"Mr. Justice . . ." It was Toby Ellis. "Look back up on the trail. Near the basalt outcropping. High up."

Ruff followed the pointing finger and he too saw them. Cheyenne. He got quickly to his feet.

"Let's move it."

They emerged from the canyon to stand on the sunny flats. It was like another world, this land that did not uptilt and crumble away, that did not offer the chance of death with each step wrongly placed.

Or did it? Maybe it was more dangerous by far than the bluff and its snaking trail.

"Let's get moving and keep moving," Ruff said. "Toby and Reb, you might check over your weapons as we move."

Ruff started out then, Dawn Sky at his side. Rudy Stuyvestant, who had been very quiet since the epi-

sode on the cliff, followed, then the soldiers. Reb
Saunders, holding that captured Indian rifle across
his body, came last. Reb's hat was tugged low, his face
grim as he looked constantly behind them, hobbling
along in his ill-fitting cavalry boots, boots that had
already worn great puffy blisters on his feet.

The day seemed warm on the flats, and as they
trudged on it grew warmer. Sweat trickled down Ruff's
throat, stung his eyes, soaked his back.

"The coulee," Dawn Sky said, pointing. "There, Ruff
Justice."

"All right," he agreed. Ruff turned his head toward
the others and pointed. The coulee, gouged out of the
prairie by short-lived freshets, was invisible from any
distance. If they could travel along the bottom of the
wash, they might elude detection for a time longer,
maybe enough to make a difference. Every chance had
to be utilized now, every opportunity to gain minutes,
hours.

The coulee was shallow, ten feet deep, with sandy
shoulders. No water ran in the channel although silver-
green willows flourished in some areas. The insects
were heavy; mosquitoes swarmed over them, cicadas
sang in the brush. They tramped on, the going difficult in the sand, the day warm and airless in the
coulee bottom.

They found the first horse a mile on.

It was Dryer who found it, and he was afraid to
mention it at first. He thought he was suffering from
hallucinations. Something of deep brown coloration
moving through the willows. It took on definition before Dryer's swollen, mosquito-plagued eyes, becoming a horse's muscular haunch. An army bay was
what it was, and he nearly forgot himself and shouted
out in his excitement.

"Hold up," he hissed to Reb Saunders, and the corporal whistled softly to Justice.

Ruff halted and jogged back to where the two soldiers stood examining the horse. It wore a U.S. brand, looked gaunt and bedraggled; its saddle had slipped sideways.

"One of yours," Ruff said.

"Yes," Dryer said, touching the smear of dried blood on the horse's flank, "it is."

"Not much good for riding just now. It won't carry all of us anyway."

"It's a horse. Straighten the saddle around and bring it on."

And the second one was fifty yards on. It too was an army bay, and it looked up at them with bewildered, hopeful eyes. Its hooves had cut the reins to ribbons as it trampled on them. It seemed sound, only well-worn.

"They don't do us much good," Rudy Stuyvestant said pessimistically.

"No, but they're something."

"Maybe someone could ride for help at Morgan Creek," Toby Ellis said. "I'd volunteer."

"There wouldn't be much help there," Reb Saunders told him. "A mining town. How you going to talk people into riding out here to save our necks?"

"Lincoln . . ." But Lincoln was too damned far, just too far.

They walked on, wondering when the Cheyenne would come, knowing with certainty that they would. From time to time Justice or Reb would scramble up the sandy bluffs and peer out onto the long flats, looking, just looking. So far they had seen no sign of Eagle Spirit. So far the coulee had continued deep enough, westward enough, to help them. Neither condition could last forever.

"Mr. Justice!"

Toby Ellis trotted forward to where Ruff trudged on. Now the scout stopped and turned.

"What is it?"

"You might think I'm crazy, but I heard something." The soldier hesitated. "A man calling for help—in English. It seemed to be coming from up there, to the south."

"You're daydreaming now," Dryer said. "No one could be out here."

"The horses were here," Toby said, and that closed the argument.

"Let's have us a look," Ruff Justice said.

"Mr. Justice . . . it could be a Cheyenne trick."

"Yes," Justice agreed. "And it might not be. If there's someone up there, we've got to have our look."

"I'm damned if I'll go," Rudy Stuyvestant said. The heat, the long trek, had brought back his scratchy disposition.

"You don't have to," Justice said.

"If one of us goes up, we risk being seen, isn't that right?" Rudy demanded.

"That's right."

"What right have you got to risk all our lives for one man?"

"No right at all. It's just the way it's going to be. You want to brace me about this too, Rudy?" Ruff asked, and his eyes went cold and hard.

"No." Rudy's eyes shifted away. "I guess not."

Justice climbed with Reb to the rim of the coulee and for long minutes they lay against the hot sand, looking out onto the dry grass plains. Some hundred yards away was a stand of gnarled oaks growing among ancient gray boulders. Otherwise there was nothing visible on all the long plains.

"Has to be coming from the trees," Reb said.

"Yes. Cover me with that rifle . . . for all the good it will do."

"Ruff Justice . . ." Dawn Sky touched his arm and shook her head pleadingly.

"It has to be done, woman; it is a matter of honor."

"I know. Be careful."

"Sure." Sure, be careful on the wide plains, walking into a Cheyenne trap while behind you the army of ghost walkers closed in. "I'll be careful."

He glanced at Reb, who nodded, then slipped up onto the flats, trotting toward the trees, his eyes moving constantly. Nothing. He saw nothing but a lone soaring eagle against the clearing skies.

But he heard the cry again. A long, anguished cry. It could have been a Cheyenne calling them to him; they were very good at that trick, and Ruff had seen many a man suckered by it; but he didn't think so. He just didn't think that type of agony could be faked.

But then he had been wrong many times before.

He was fully exposed as he crossed the flats, but then the shadows of the big oaks flickered across his eyes and he was into them, the silence comforting after the expectation of violence.

Old man Stuyvestant lay folded up in the rocks, his face battered, one leg twisted crazily. There was blood flowing from his nostrils, blood dried on his ears.

"Justice . . ." The voice was weak.

"What happened?"

"The boy?" Stuyvestant asked, clutching at Ruff's shirt as he knelt down beside him, examining the wounds.

"He's all right. Rudy's alive."

"A man don't like to go out leaving nothin' . . . you know, Justice?"

"He's all right. What happened?"

"Ralston. Ralston and the woman. We made it out

of there with the gold. We were ready to run, you see. Had it all in a wagon, horses hitched—oxen too slow—when the Cheyenne came in, we left ... fast. Kid okay?"

"He's okay."

"Wanted to take him, but Ralston said no. We got plenty rich, huh? We found it all. Big cache. Lot of dust ... now Ralston's got it."

"Norah's all right?"

"All right ... damned she-devil. She helped him. They beat me and left me for dead. Guess I damned near ..." He didn't say any more. His mouth and eyes gaped open. The flies began to descend. Ruff Justice rose and shook his head, taking a slow breath. Death by greed. He had seen it often, too often. He searched the body and found an empty purse and a silver watch. He tucked the watch into his pocket.

Then he took off, running toward the coulee again, looking behind him as he ran, and then to the east. To the east, and he saw them coming. A mile and a half off, perhaps. But they were coming. Half a hundred painted Cheyenne.

Ruff Justice slid into the coulee, spraying dust and sand on the men below. Dawn Sky rushed to him to hold his arm.

"Cheyenne coming," Ruff said tersely. "Let's get moving."

"They saw you!" Rudy Stuyvestant spun Ruff around. "They saw you and they know where we are."

"Likely."

"And for what! For what?" the kid hissed. "Was there anyone up there, anyone worth risking our necks for?"

"Just a dying man," Justice said. He wiped the sweat from his eyes. "He's dead now. Gone." Ruff handed Rudy Stuyvestant the silver watch, his father's watch, and turned away, leaving the kid to stare at his back. "Let's move it. Fast!"

"Stuyvestant?" Reb asked as they jogged along the coulee bottom.

"Yeah. How'd you know?"

"Guessed when I saw the kid's face." Reb shook his head. "What happened?"

Ruff told him all he knew, which wasn't much. Saunders grew furious. "An officer. Our officer! Didn't have anything in mind but getting the gold, did he?"

"It seems not. Nor did the girl. They deserve each other."

"Ruff—how many Cheyenne back there?"

Justice glanced at the corporal and told him, "Too many, Reb. Too damned many."

"No chance at all?"

"I don't see it if there is."

"Damn," Reb Saunders said, and then his jaw clamped shut. They ran on, the heat growing intense. They ran on knowing that the Cheyenne were closing the gap all the while.

The coulee was narrowing, closing around them as they approached the series of low bluffs ahead. It didn't matter about the coulee any longer. They had been seen; they would be found.

"If we can get into the bluffs, at least we'll have the high ground," Reb Saunders said. Ruff just nodded as the two men jogged on.

"That's some help," Rudy Stuyvestant said sarcastically. "We have the high ground—and they got us a hundred to one. We got two rifles and Justice's six-gun. But we get the high ground!"

"Stuyvestant," Reb Saunders snapped, "I'm getting damned tired of you. Beats the hell out of me why Mr. Justice hasn't cut you loose to take care of yourself. He's saved your damn worthless life for you twice, took care of your daddy in his dyin' when you didn't have the guts to go to him. You got any better ideas, why don't you just go off somewhere and do 'em. Otherwise, keep your fat mouth shut."

"Mr. Justice!"

Toby Ellis yelled out and Ruff, running steadily, his eyes on the bluffs ahead, cursed and slowed. "What is it?"

"It's . . ." Ellis strangled on his dry, thick tongue. "You best come and look."

"There ain't time for lookin' at anything!" Dryer complained; then he said, "Oh, Jesus . . ."

By that time Ruff was to them, looking down at the twisted broken thing that had been a woman, had been Norah Gates. The wagon was on its side farther back in the brush. Scattered around the ground were sacks of gold dust, one of them burst to show its yellow glitter.

"Cheyenne got her," Dryer said.

"Wrong guess," Justice said. Something had gotten her, mauled her like a panther. Something as savage as a Cheyenne, something that enjoyed the hurting. "I should have killed him in Minneapolis," Justice said under his breath. "I could see it in his eyes. He's done this before. Many times, maybe."

"Who's done it, Mr. Justice?"

"Lieutenant Ralston."

"Done this?" Reb looked at the woman's battered body, at the bruised face, the torn dress, the skirt hiked up over her waist, the dried blood caked in the honey-colored hair. "Lieutenant Ralston?"

"He did it, dammit, Reb. I don't want to argue about it!" Justice snarled. Saunders hadn't ever seen the scout in that kind of temper. Justice's blue eyes were hard and cold, his mouth was twisted savagely. He was a killing thing and Red Saunders instinctively backed away a step.

"Ruff Justice," Dawn Sky said, touching his arm. "We must be going now. There is nothing to do for her now."

"No." Ruff shook it off. "She's right, let's get up onto the bluffs. Maybe we can hold them back for a while."

"What about the girl?"

"Can't take the time to bury her."

"The gold." Rudy Stuyvestant looked around at the dust, strewn about the sandy bottom of the coulee.

"If you want to carry it along, you go ahead and collect it up, Stuyvestant. Your daddy thought it was worth dying for; do you?"

Stuyvestant didn't answer, but when Ruff led out again up the sandy wash, he was behind him and his arms were empty. Justice was no longer thinking about Rudy and his gold. Nor was he, at that moment, thinking about the Cheyenne behind them.

He was thinking of one thing, of vengeance, and as he ran his eyes were fixed on the ground beneath his feet. It showed quite clearly the boot prints of another man—the tracks of Neil Ralston, a twisted thing, which must die.

15.

They were out of the wash and climbing, climbing the bluffs, which at no point were more than fifty feet high and in most places were much less. Sage and sumac grew there and an occasional low, wind-twisted, weather-stunted cedar. There were deep shadows gathering in the ravines now and along the foot of the bluffs. The sun was sinking slowly, reddening, growing large and misty against the western sky.

The Cheyenne were coming on. Steadily, patiently now. They had their quarry and they knew it.

Ruff Justice had his as well. He was the hunted, but also the hunter. A dark, savage hunter, as determined and bloodthirsty as the Cheyenne behind him.

"He's hurt," Ruff said.

"What is this, Ruff Justice?" Dawn Sky whispered as they climbed the sandy slopes and emerged from the ravine to stand panting on the low bluff, looking out across the dusk-purpled prairie behind them.

"Ralston."

"The soldier who killed the girl?"

"That's right." Ruff was crouched down, his finger touching the dark stain on a lichen-crusted rock. He lifted his finger to his tongue and tasted the blood, nodding. "That wagon rolled and threw him. Norah was already dead. He's running heavy now. He's hurt and he's carrying gold."

"Justice, we got Indians to worry about," Toby Ellis said anxiously.

"No sense worrying about them. We'll fight them as long and as well as we can." Justice rose and Ellis could only stare. Since finding the girl's body, the man had gone utterly cold. Justice stood looking across the bluff toward a rocky sinkhole a hundred yards on. There, stacked boulders formed a wall on three sides. In the bottom of the sink there might be some water. A small force could do worse than to make its stand there.

"Could be," Justice said to himself.

"What could be, dammit?" Stuyvestant demanded.

"We'll fort up in that depression," Ruff said. Below them there was suddenly the familiar yipping of war cries. Still distant, but excited and chilling. Looking that way, they saw the long line of Cheyenne warriors spread out across the dark grassy plain, their horses urged on into a run as they again spotted the party of whites.

"Let's do what we're going to do damned quick," Toby Ellis said.

"Let us make a run for it," Dryer pleaded. "There's two horses. Me and Toby can make it to Morgan Creek."

Reb Saunders shook his head. "You'll never make it on those animals, Dryer. Do as Mr. Justice says."

"Reb!"

"No. That's it, Private Dryer!"

"We might as well cut the horses loose then," Albright said, speaking for the first time in a long, long while.

"No." Justice turned to the kid. "We might get damned hungry if this lasts."

Dawn Sky stood beside Justice, looking up at him, seeing the determination in the set of his jaw. He cut a tall lean figure against the red of sunset. His long hair drifted in the wind. His eyes were fixed and implacable. She alone perhaps understood him at that moment. The wish for peace, the need to do violence, the casual appraisal of his own onrushing death. Dawn Sky stood beside him and watched as he watched, and when he started off, his long-striding form moving toward the sinkhole, she kept the others back.

"Wait here."

"Wait here, hell. What's he doing? Has he gone mad!"

"No need to listen to the squaw. I'm not going to stand here and wait for them."

"Holy Christ," Reb Saunders said in a whisper. It had come to him what Justice was going to do, why he wanted the others to wait behind. "He's up there. Ralston's up there in the sinkhole."

The soldiers looked at each other and then started forward, Dawn Sky grabbing futilely at their arms as they passed.

Rudy Stuyvestant, frowning, spoke before he followed. "They'll have to stop him. He may be right, but Ralston's their superior officer. They'll have to stop him."

"No one can," Dawn Sky said.

"Then they'll kill him, little woman. You understand that? They'll kill Ruff Justice."

Then the woman too took off running toward the sinkhole and Rudy Stuyvestant was left behind, cursing the day he was born, looking back down the bluff to where the Cheyenne, painted and hostile, were dismounting from their war ponies and rushing forward. Without a weapon Rudy couldn't do a damn thing. He began running toward the sinkhole himself, his legs leaden, his heart stony. It was nearly dark, he told himself as he searched for scant comfort. Maybe they won't come after dark—though Justice said they didn't mind fighting at night, it was just that they didn't want their horses hurt. Cavalry isn't much good at night . . . *still,* maybe they wouldn't come. This was a holy war, wasn't it? They must believe in all that about losing your soul in the darkness—or was any of that true?

He reached the sinkhole and clambered in over the waist-high rocks. In the bottom of the depression stood Ruff Justice, the soldiers around him. On the ground the officer sat looking up at them all.

"You killed her." Ruff Justice's voice was heavy and sober.

"She was killed when the wagon rolled," Neil Ralston said. His eyes were black in the shadows. There was a heavy bruise on the side of his face. His ankle was badly swollen. He had made the mistake of cutting his boot away from it. Beside him was a canteen, a Winchester rifle, and four sacks of gold dust.

"You're a goddamned liar. Make your stand," Ruff Justice said coldly.

"What the hell's the matter with you! I told you what happened. Corporal, disarm this civilian. That's an order. Ruff Justice is mad."

"Sir, I—"

"You heard me, didn't you? Is this mutiny? That's a capital offense, isn't it, Corporal Saunders? You other men are witnesses to this. Now, again, Corporal Saunders, I am ordering you to arrest this civilian."

"Sir, he says you killed a woman."

"I know what he says, damn you, but it's a lie! You would take his side against me? The whole lot of you will end before a firing squad."

"Mr. Justice . . ."

"Sorry, Reb. He dies," Ruff answered.

"Corporal Saunders, I'm warning you!"

"Yes, sir. I know it, sir. I just don't know . . ."

Johnny Albright came forward, looked down at the officer, and said, "After what we've been through, you'd listen to this man, Reb? Hell, ask him where he was while we were fighting the Cheyenne back at the Heart. Ask him where he's heading with that gold." Albright spat. "I wouldn't trust him to kick a dog for me. And it won't do much good for you to threaten me with a firing squad, Lieutenant Ralston. They've already got something like that planned for me. Stand back, Reb, and let Justice do what needs to be done."

"I can't . . ." Reb Saunders began, but before he could finish his sentence Ralston made his choice.

He was smooth about it, very smooth, and it came at an unexpected moment. Beneath his thigh was a Schofield revolver, and as Justice turned his head a quarter away to look at Reb, the officer yanked the gun out. Dawn Sky screamed and Ruff threw himself to one side as the revolver in Ralston's hand spoke with deadly intent. Ruff hit the ground on his shoulder and rolled. When he came up, Ralston's muzzle was still trained on him, but Justice had his long-barreled Colt in his hand. He fired from one knee as the renegade officer squeezed off another round, which whistled past Ruff's ear to whine off the rocks behind.

Ruff's bullet didn't miss. It took Ralston at the base of the throat and tore his neck open, slamming the officer backward, the blood spewing from the gaping wound. He was dead before he hit the ground, his spinal cord severed by the .44-caliber bullet.

"Here they come, by God!"

The voice was Dryer's. The soldier waved an arm frantically and the others rushed to the wall. Albright had Ralston's handgun, Stuyvestant his Winchester. As they reached the wall of stone above, they saw the first wave of Cheyenne make their charge across the bluff.

Ruff Justice waited, his Colt at arm's length, sighting down the long barrel. A rifle in the hands of a Cheyenne spat flame and the bullet came too near to Justice. Still he didn't move. To his left someone fired. A hit or a miss, Ruff didn't know. He had his eyes on his chosen target, his alternate target, and that was all that mattered. His concentration was complete.

A dozen Cheyenne were in the first rank, a dozen more behind. They were painted devils moving through the shadows of dusk, rifles held high or fired from the waist, war cries shrilling.

Ruff Justice fired his first shot and the war cry died in a Cheyenne brave's throat. He shifted his sights to his second target and squeezed off again, hearing the close explosion of bullets as his own side fired a volley. Saunders had them under control; the ammunition wasn't being wasted; all of them had been in enough fights to know that every round had to count.

Ruff saw a Cheyenne in a war bonnet crumple and go down, saw another with yellow and black snakes painted on his legs and arms get hit, roll, and crawl away into the greasewood and sage on his right.

But where was Eagle Spirit? What did he look like? Was he with this group or was he back at the war camp?

Ruff fired again, saw his shot miss and, cursing, he began popping the empty cartridges from his Colt. He reloaded quickly, each small movement long-practiced, too often used.

Reb Saunders fired again and his shot was echoed by Toby Ellis's. Suddenly the field was empty. There were six dead warriors out there, their shadows merging with the shadows gathering beneath the sagebrush, but the living were gone, the attack abruptly ended.

"What happened?" Rudy Stuyvestant asked.

Ruff shook his head. "I'm not sure. Dawn Sky?"

"I do not know. I think they must do magic now."

"It's dark," Stuyvestant said, pursuing his thought. "Maybe they won't be coming in again."

Again Ruff had to look a question at Dawn Sky, but even she did not know. "He does what his spirit tells him to do."

"They've counted our guns," Reb Saunders put in. "Counted them and measured us. When they come again it'll be a lot more than what they showed us here."

"That's what it was," Ellis guessed. "Counting our guns. That Eagle Spirit just threw away the lives of them out there."

A horse nickered behind them and their heads turned in unison. He still lay there. Dark, unmoving.

"Someone bury Ralston," Saunders said. "Dryer? Albright."

"Sure."

The two soldiers moved off into the sinkhole. Reb watched them for a while and then his eyes met Ruff's in the near-darkness.

"What do we tell them, Mr. Justice? If we get out of here, I mean? They'll have me up in front of the wall and you'll be swinging from the Bismarck gallows. We disobeyed a direct order under fire and watched you shoot him down."

"I wouldn't worry about it," Ruff said grimly. There wasn't much point in worrying about anything that was going to happen if they got out of there alive. The odds on that were so remote as to not bear consideration.

"No," Reb said softly. "You're right."

"Water?"

Ruff turned, smiling. Dawn Sky had brought the canteen to him. He sat down, wiping his forehead with the back of his sleeve. She was there, close and caring in the darkness. He could see only a razor-thin band of deep red against the sky, and by that light he studied her features as she gave him a drink from the canteen.

"Thank you."

"You will have more?"

"Save it for the others."

"Yes," she said, "I will do that."

"Sit down beside me, Dawn Sky," Ruff said, and she did so, looking up into his eyes.

"What is it, Ruff Justice?"

"I want you to go. Just walk on out of here. There's a horse if you want it. I don't think any of the others could make it out, but you might."

"You want me to go to this Morgan Creek for help?"

"No. There's no help going to come, Dawn Sky. You know that. It's too far to any help."

"You want . . . I will not leave you!"

"Dawn Sky . . ." He took her hand but she yanked it away.

"No! A true woman would not leave her man."

"There's no point in you dying."

"I will not go."

Ruff nodded. It wasn't going to do any good to argue; she had her mind made up. They sat side by side, not speaking. There were no sounds but the muttered words of the men below, the distant calling of an owl.

"What is he doing?" Ruff wondered out loud. What was Eagle Spirit doing now?

"Speaking to them, telling them what must be done," Dawn Sky answered, knowing who Ruff meant.

"Magic."

"Yes"—she shrugged—"magic."

Ruff was silent for a minute. "And if there was no magic?"

"What do you mean?"

"If there was no magic. If all of what he is telling them is a lie? If his magic isn't strong enough to save him."

"What are you thinking!" Dawn Sky got to her knees and put her fingers to Ruff's lips as if to stifle the words and thereby the thoughts behind the words. "No!"

"Why not? What other chance is there?"

"We can run."

"No farther. We are too slow." He took her hand and kissed the palm then smiled. "I've got to go down into their camp. I've got to kill Eagle Spirit before the sun rises. I've got to destroy him and destroy his magic."

"No, it is madness."

"It's the only way."

"I will go to him again. I will beg him. I will tell him that I will do anything," Dawn Sky said pleadingly.

"That won't do any good and you know it. You'll just get yourself hurt."

"I will do anything—"

"There's nothing to be done!" Justice said with sudden anger. Nothing but to go down there and do it. Kill the magician, and with him the magic that called for blood, promised victory over the more numerous white guns.

"Ruff Justice . . ."

"Won't you go away? Alone you can slip out of here, go back north to the reservation."

"Not without you. What do you think I am?"

"A friend," he answered. "A very good friend."

"And no more?"

He smiled and put his arm around her. "Yes, a little more."

"Then I will not go. But you must not go down into Eagle Spirit's camp."

"No? You've asked me, now I'll ask you: what do you think *I* am?"

"Do not ask me." Her head turned away.

"What?" He took her chin and turned her face to him. "What am I?"

"A warrior, Ruff Justice. You are a warrior."

"And so it must be done."

"Yes." Her voice was only a dry whisper. "When will you go then, Ruff Justice?"

"Soon." It would have to be soon. Before Eagle Spirit had finished with his magic, before he sent his overpowering force against the small band of soldiers. Before the hour had passed, before the low, softly glowing moon had risen another degree in the cold and inky sky.

He put his arm around the woman again and she scooted close to him to sit there in the darkness, neither speaking, letting the last minutes slip away.

16.

Ruff found Reb Saunders and told him what he was going to try. The soldier shook his head in the darkness. His voice was weary and gritty when he answered.

"Ruff, I reckon they'll kill you."

"Reb, I reckon you're right, but there's a chance, and there's none if we sit and wait."

"No, none at all," the corporal said. "I figured on bunching our guns along the southern wall here like we were before. Maybe put Dryer up on the flank just in case the—"

"Mr. Justice! Mr. Justice!"

It was Toby Ellis who called out and then came up at a trot, hatless, his rifle in hand.

"Are they coming?"

"No, it's not that. The girl—she's gone."

"Gone! Dawn Sky?"

"Yes, sir. I was standing watch and I seen her just climb up and over the wall and start walking across the flats toward the Indian camp. I didn't call out in case ı gave her away to someone, but . . ."

Justice was already walking away from Ellis, grinding his teeth together. Damn the woman! She didn't mind worth a damn. She had some idea about talking Eagle Spirit out of this slaughter, about saving Ruff's life, and all that was going to happen was that she was going to get herself killed.

"What's up?" Rudy Stuyvestant asked. Justice didn't answer. He clambered up the natural wall himself and then was gone, slipping into the darkness. Ahead of him the fire from the Cheyenne camp danced against the cobalt sky. To the east the big white moon was rising, a mocking, challenging moon.

Ruff kept to the verge of the brush, not wanting to walk through it because of the noise, or to abandon it altogether. His shadowy figure was lost against the background of sage and manzanita. The scent of the sage and the dew-heavy grass was rich in his nostrils.

The moon showed him a sentry hunkered down on his heels staring off toward the east, toward his home perhaps, when he should have been watching the tiny force of whites. Ruff was to him in four steps, raising the butt of his Colt and crashing it down behind the Cheyenne's ear.

Quickly then Justice returned to the shadows, working his way up a rocky ravine toward the firelight, which now glowed against the sky like a great beacon. The drums were loud, the sound of chanting was audible. They were making a party of it, and why not? There was no possibility of defeat. There would be plenty of time for Eagle Spirit to work his magic, to indulge his whims, to peel skulls and shatter bones . . .

Ruff was up out of the ravine and there he was: standing on the perimeter of the Indian war camp staring at the fire, at the dancers, at the men sitting around the fire talking, drinking.

And then there was silence, sudden and complete. Justice thought at first that he had been spotted and his body tensed, every cord and sinew, every fiber of muscle, going taut and dry.

He saw then what it was. Dawn Sky had brought the silence with her from the shadows. She walked across the camp and in silence the men watched her.

A knot in a fire log crackled loudly as it burned and the noise was like a shot in the stillness.

The warriors fell back and Ruff saw him for the first time. Buffalo horns decorated the head of Eagle Spirit. He had black circles painted around his eyes, and in the hollows of his cheeks more dark paint had been smeared to create a skull's head. He was tall, very tall for a Cheyenne, naked but for a breechclout. In his hand was a war hatchet, a handful of feathers tied to its handle near the head. The buffalo hide, which was draped down his back, had bones sewn into it. They were human bones.

"Eagle Spirit, husband!" Dawn Sky cried out in English. She walked to him, her hands stretched out. "The Lord loves you."

The hatchet flashed through the air and was buried in Dawn Sky's heart. She didn't make another sound. She fell to the dark earth and lay there.

"Treacherous thing," Eagle Spirit said. His voice was a breathy growl.

"Eagle Spirit?"

The speaker was a white man. Eagle Spirit turned slowly toward the voice, his dark eyes glinting with firelight and expectation. The man standing before him was tall, his hair long and dark. He was dressed in buckskins.

"Who are you?"

"The dark spirit," Ruff Justice answered.

"What are you talking about!" Eagle Spirit threw back his head and roared with laughter, the muscles of his throat bulging. "You are only the dead walking," the Cheyenne warlord said finally.

"So are we all," Ruff Justice said. "But your time has come. You will die tonight. I am the dark spirit come to claim you."

The Cheyenne warriors who were gathered around

said nothing. They watched, waiting for Eagle Spirit to strike this white warrior down, to demonstrate the power that his spirits had given to him.

"Throw off your robe," Ruff said. "I have come to test the strength of my spirit against yours."

"Take him and kill him," Eagle Spirit said carelessly. Several of the Cheyenne started eagerly forward. Ruff shouted at them.

"Wait! You are risking your fates on this man's magic. You are entering a war trusting to his spirits. I say his spirits are lies. They are nothing but the dreams of a madman. If they are true spirits, then let him strike me down. Me alone! If Eagle Spirit cannot do that, how can he lead you into a war of conquest?" Apparently enough of the Cheyenne understood his English words for the warriors to stop as a group, and wait.

"I have nothing to prove," Eagle Spirit said. There was an edge to his voice. He was ready all right, ready to do the job himself. Maybe he only thought it was beneath his dignity to kill this single white man, this buckskinned scout.

"You have nothing left to prove, no," Justice said. "You have shown you are a coward, a woman-killer, a fake, a liar. . . ."

Eagle Spirit bellowed with rage. He leaped through the air, his buffalo robe and horns falling from his lithe, cat-quick body. Justice threw himself to one side, seeing the fire-burnished ax head slice air beside him as he hit the ground and rolled away.

Eagle Spirit was quick and he was a fighting man, a man who had lived by his weapons. Now that the first flush of rage had burned away, he became methodical, more deadly by far than the wildly attacking madman he had seemed at first.

Ruff had his bowie knife in his hand. He backed and

circled, aware of the hot crackling fire behind him, of the watching dark eyes of the Cheyenne warriors, of the pale moon beaming down from out of the inky sky.

And before him was the madman, the killer of women, the bloody-handed thing. There were still dark stains on the war hatchet in Eagle Spirit's hand. Dark stains that had been the life of a young woman.

It infuriated Ruff, angered him beyond hatred and vengeance lust. The coldness had returned to him as it had to Eagle Spirit. He would kill this man. Kill him and then perhaps the Cheyenne would tear him to pieces—that didn't matter. Nothing mattered but eliminating this thing, this beast that stalked the plains hungering for fresh kill like a mad wolf.

Eagle Spirit came in, cut right with his hatchet, and was met by Ruff's knife blade. Steel rang against steel as Justice blocked the blow and stepped back, nearer to the roaring fire. Eagle Spirit kicked out, trying for Ruff's groin, but Justice crossed a thigh over, blocking the effort. Ruff slashed at the Indian's throat, but Eagle Spirit was able to avoid the knife's point.

A low sound had begun to build, a sound Ruff at first could not identify. Then he heard and understood. The Cheyenne warriors were standing, chanting a death song. It was a communal prayer, a common demand for the blood of Ruff Justice.

Eagle Spirit tried to cause it to flow for them. He came in with the ax, going for the hands that Ruff kept in close to his body now. His right feinted with the bowie enough to keep Eagle Spirit back on his heels, off balance, then Justice's foot went out, back-heeling the Cheyenne.

Eagle Spirit tripped and went down. The chanting stopped as Justice rushed in, wanting to take advantage of the trip, wanting to finish it.

But the Cheyenne warlord was quick. He had gone down hard on his back, driving the breath from his body, but he was alert enough to roll away as Ruff's knife slashed at the air beside his head.

He wasn't quick enough to keep Ruff Justice from hooking his arm with his left hand.

As Eagle Spirit tried to rise, Justice pulled him back and the Cheyenne, off balance, stumbled and went down. Justice was on top of him like a mauling cougar, his knee driving up into the warrior's groin. Eagle Spirit grunted with pain and tried to bury his war ax in Ruff's face.

He was a second too slow. Ruff's bowie arced upward and out, the razor-edged blade catching flesh, severing the tendons in Eagle Spirit's wrist. With a cry of pain, the ax fell free.

The Cheyenne went wild with fury and fear. He bucked beneath Ruff Justice, clawing at his eyes, his own dark, skull-painted face taunt with mad anger.

He was there, a living, raging, dark-eyed, soulless beast, a killing, clawing, nerveless creature who lived only to bring death to others. He was there and then he was not. The bowie was drawn back and then driven home, deep into the throat of the invincible one, the man who rode with the spirits, the warlord who could not be killed except by magic.

That was what he had told them: that only magic could take his life. He was invincible to all that was human. He had lied; either Eagle Spirit had lied or the tall man in buckskins, who now rose from the ground where the dead warlord lay, was himself a magician. Had he not said he brought the dark spirit with him?

He did not look at them; they did not move.

He walked to where the dead woman lay, and he scooped Dawn Sky up in his strong arms. Then, without looking left or right, he started out of the camp, walking into the face of the huge, cold Cheyenne moon, which rose from the plains. No hand was lifted to halt the white man, no one called out a warning. He was gone, that was all. Eagle Spirit was dead and the white man had just walked away.

There is nothing to do when a war is ended, and so the Cheyenne packed their war bags and mounted their ponies and rode away out onto the dark and empty plains, leaving the fire burning behind them, the funeral pyre of the dead one, the one whose magic was not strong enough.

"They're pulling out! Damn me, boys, they're pulling out!" Rudy Stuyvestant shouted, breaking into a little jig as exultation washed over him. "Look at 'em go . . . damn it all, look at 'em!"

Reb Saunders placed his fingers to his lips and shook his head.

"What's the matter? Oh . . ." Rudy looked across the sinkhole to where the scout sat. He just sat there and on his lap was the head of the dead girl. He rested his hand on her dark hair and looked up at the soldiers, at Stuyvestant, saying nothing.

"Think I should apologize?" Rudy asked. Reb shook his head.

"Just leave him alone."

"Also," Toby Ellis put in, "you might quit that whoopin' and dancin'. Them Cheyenne are just liable to come back."

They didn't, however. Reb and the others sat up the night through clinging to their cold weapons, watching the shadows drift and change as the moon swung over. The Cheyenne fire burned low and dawn began to break. The Indians were gone.

"Well," Dryer said, "he's buried her. I thought he

was going to sit there and keep holding her till she rotted, but he's buried her—and look at that, he gave her a Christian marker."

"The woman was a mission Christian," Albright said.

"Was she? Well he buried her and put a cross up. Smoothed out one side of the crosspiece and wrote somethin' on it. Her name, I expect."

"I expect," Reb Saunders answered. It wasn't until an hour later when they started out eastward, toward Fort Lincoln far in the distance, that Reb took a look at the marker Ruff Justice had put over the rock cairn that covered Dawn Sky's grave.

He had smoothed out one face of the crosspiece and laboriously carved into it: "Dawn Sky—She Was a True Woman."

17.

"Lieutenant Ralston was murdered!"

Colonel MacEnroe was furious. He stood with his hands behind his back, glowering at Ruff Justice, who sat in the corner chair, his long legs crossed lazily, his hat perched on his knee.

"When did you hear?"

"A day after you left, Ruff. I recalled what you said about checking up on Lieutenant Neil Ralston. I know you had something against him and it got to worrying me. Your instincts are usually good ones."

"What did you do, sir, wire Fort Abercrombie?"

"I did, yes. I felt a little foolish about it, but when I got the answer to my wire, I was more than embarrassed, I was angry. I'd sent that man out with you and one of my patrols. I'd been completely taken in!"

"What happened to the real Lieutenant Ralston?" Ruff asked.

"Murdered, as I said. How, why, no one knows. But he was murdered by this man whose name appears to be Henry Fitch—they're still checking on that. Murdered, clothing exchanged, and Fitch came on to Lincoln to begin an army career. Incredible," MacEnroe said, "incredible that he could fool me."

"Not really. Probably they'll find that Fitch had military experience. There's very few men wandering around these days that haven't seen some army service on one side or the other."

"Well, that's true. Still, I feel the fool, Ruffin."

"He's gone now, sir. It's over."

"Yes, it's over," MacEnroe said in a tone that implied it was never over: the fighting, the dying, the bloodshed. Not on the Dakota plains. The colonel sat at his desk and pulled out the bourbon bottle, pouring a tall drink. "I didn't recognize that Stuyvestant kid. What did you do to him, Ruff?"

"Rudy?" Justice shrugged. "He's got good stuff in him; he just gets a little puffed up now and then. I think he saw the elephant out there. He'll be all right."

"You saw the report on Norah Gates?"

"I saw it. She wasn't quite what we thought either, was she?"

"A notorious gambler. Blackmail. Extortion. A clever little confidence woman. She ran one game too many, it seems."

"They always do." Ruff watched the colonel finish his drink. There was one unresolved bit of business he hesitated to bring up. Hesitated because it mattered to him. There was still a life at stake here, and it was Ruff's responsibility.

"What is it, Ruffin?" the colonel asked.

"Johnny Albright."

"You must have heard by now: Joe Gordon pulled through. Dr. Simms, despite the rumors, is a good surgeon."

"So Albright won't be charged with murder?"

"No. As a matter of fact," the colonel said, suppressing a smile, "he won't be charged."

"He what?"

"General Hewitt is the regimental judge advocate. At this moment on his desk is a recommendation from

General Stafford that Albright be shown leniency. In the face of the enemy Private John J. Albright exhibited uncommon courage and has won the right of exoneration through valor. Old army tradition, you know." The colonel filled his glass again.

"Wonder who advised General Stafford of Albright's valor in the face of the enemy," Justice said dryly.

"Well," the colonel said with a shrug, "he's a good kid. I don't mean to let him off entirely—don't take me for a soft man, Justice!" MacEnroe warned the scout.

"No, sir."

"He's got six months of company punishment coming to him—the worst details Sergeant Pierce can think of. Albright will be on every blessed one!"

"Yes, sir," Ruff Justice said. He did everything he could to hold back the smile, but when he left the colonel's office, he was still smiling. He said good day to Mack Pierce and went on out into the clear, harsh light of day to stand on the plankwalk before the orderly room, looking toward the broad, silver Missouri and the plains, pale green and red brown, running away to the end of the earth. And then he found himself thinking about her, and the smile slowly fell away.

Ruff Justice walked slowly across the parade ground toward the paddock opposite. He meant to saddle a horse and ride it—to ride it far and fast, to ride it long and let the cold winds cleanse him, strip her memory from him and scatter it across the prairies where it would lie and abide and endure.

WESTWARD HO!

The following is the opening chapter from the next novel in the gun-blazing, action-packed new Ruff Justice series from Signet:

RUFF JUSTICE #16: HIGH VENGEANCE

1.

The door swung open and the fury of the Rocky Mountain blizzard swept into the dark, damp room. The tall man's silhouette filled the doorway briefly and then he staggered in, the door banging shut behind him.

There were six men in the store, which doubled as a saloon in this tiny Colorado mountain town. Almost in unison their heads had turned to the newcomer, their eyes measuring him.

It was apparent immediately that something was wrong. No one in his right mind would be out and about in this weather, not without a compelling reason.

"Are you all right?" Ned Stokes asked. He was the proprietor of the sod-roofed, smoky store. Even inside, Stokes wore his big buffalo coat. The heat from the iron stove in the corner never reached him behind the counter, where he worked selling his home-cooked liquor. "I said, are you all right?"

The tall man stumbled across the room, moving toward the stove, which glowed a dull cherry red. Ice fell from his feet and melted against the floor. His eyebrows and hair were whitened with frost; now that false coloration fell away and they saw that his hair was raven black, worn long.

"Ned!"

That was Andy Buehler. He had risen from the rough bench where he had been sitting sipping whiskey for two days. Now Andy's gaunt face was excited, worried. He pointed at the stained floor and Ned Stokes saw it too.

The stains the tall man was trailing behind him weren't all from snow melt. Some of it was blood.

Andy was out from behind the counter, crossing the room to where the stranger stood weaving before the stove. At the sound of Stokes's approaching footsteps he turned his head, and icy blue eyes, suddenly alert and wary, were turned on the storekeeper. Eyes that measured and then dismissed the man.

"You hurt, mister?"

"Yes. Let me sit down."

"Sure," Stokes said, "go ahead."

The stranger smiled weakly. "Would you help me?"

"Help you? Sure, all right." Stokes took the arm of the newcomer and helped him down onto the puncheon bench that ran beneath the frosted window beside the stove.

A puddle of liquid had developed beneath the tall man. Water and blood, mingling and trickling away down the crack between the two dark planks at his feet.

"You'd better have someone look at that wound."

"There's really not much point in it. Thank you anyway."

"What is it, gunshot?"

"Yes. Gunshot." Then a savage grimace twisted the stranger's face. Pain clawed at him and shook him violently. Then that too passed and he sat there pale and deathly.

"Go get Maria," he heard Stokes say. That was kind of the man. He felt sorry for Maria, whoever she was. The wound was not the kind that is pleasant to look at. It was a gut wound—the bad one was—and it had just torn him open.

Stokes was shaking his shoulder and he heard him asking, "Do you want a drink, mister? It'll help some."

He laughed, although it hurt to laugh. "No," he answered. "You see, I don't drink."

He laughed again but the pain snapped it off. He saw Stokes hovering over him, saw beyond the storekeeper other faces, all unfamiliar. He heard the sound of a woman's voice somewhere, while beside him the stove in its sandbox softly glowed, its warmth barely touching him, which was funny too, considering how far he had come just to sit beside a fire one last time before that abominable, eternal cold took him down.

She had been there at the hearth when he came back in from the bitter cold outside carrying an armload of firewood. He had seen her silhouette against the weaving red and gold flames, seen her turn to him.

"What a surprise! It's a long way to be coming in this weather."

"It was worth it. You make it worth it," she said.

"Let me put this wood down, and I'll make it worth it."

"There's no need really," she had said. Her face was in shadow but she seemed to be smiling. He was certain she was smiling.

"Is everything all right?"

"Yes, of course." Her voice was bright, but there was something wrong.

"I guess you'll be staying for supper now. It looks like it's fixing to blow again out there."

She said almost regretfully, "I won't be able to stay. There's just too much to do."

And then she lifted the gun from the folds of her skirt, the big Colt Walker pistol, which must have weighed like an anvil in her hand. She two-handed it up and the muzzle's eye, that big black horrible eye, settled on his gut. He dropped the load of firewood and took half a step backward and the big Colt thundered. He thought he screamed out her name, but he wasn't sure of that. If he had, the report of the handgun in those close quarters had drowned it out.

The bullet had tagged him hard. He knew right away that it was all over. Pain flooded his guts, like a terrible fire burning away his flesh. He staggered toward the girl but she made no move to fire again. She just stood there, as cold as the frozen woods outside, watching him.

The cabin door opened before the wind and the man with the rifle came in.

"Damn you," he said to the girl. "I told you to wait."

The injured man had ripped his long coat open and now he managed to claw his pistol out of his holster.

"Watch out!" the girl screamed, and the man in the doorway withdrew quickly as the Colt fired twice, splintering the frame of the cabin door.

One of them appeared at the window. The glass, that precious glass shipped from Denver, was broken out of the frame by the butt of a rifle and the guns spoke again. The injured man was doubled up with pain, holding his guts together with one hand, but he managed to put one cleanly into the badman's skull and he was blown away from the window.

"Roland!" The girl screamed the injured man's name. He had turned toward her, the Colt held low. He could feel the blood trickling past his waistband, down his thigh. He could barely see her for the pain that surged and then withdrew, surged again, stronger each time.

"Roland, don't shoot me!"

She dropped the gun and stepped back toward the fire. He could only look at her wistfully, wondering. There was a catch in her voice, and, he thought, tears in her eyes. He couldn't shoot her, he couldn't do her any harm.

"Why . . . ?"

She didn't answer. It was as if she couldn't answer. She stood there, young and beautiful, her fingers to her mouth, and at her feet was the ancient Colt Walker, still warm from the heat of the bullet.

"Why?" He advanced a step and stopped again, wavering. His face was contorted with pain and emotion. She just shook her head.

Her eyes grew suddenly wide and Roland turned quickly, firing as the rifleman in the doorway cut loose again. Roland missed wide. The rifle bullet struck hearthstone and plowed through the fire, kicking up ash and smoldering charcoal.

She screamed, and Roland thought she had been hit, but one glance told him that she hadn't. He wanted to take her and twist her head off, to slap her back against the wall, to take her in his arms, to do a thousand wonderful and terrible things to her.

He did none of them. He looked at her again, taking in her beauty, wondering at her treachery, and then he backed toward the window, his eyes on the door-way opposite.

In another moment he had stepped up and over the sill. The dead man lay in the snow, his dark, staring eyes gazing skyward. Roland ignored him. He started running, running toward the forest beyond, and the bullets from the cabin followed him.

He had hoped to find his horses in the sheltered cleft that nature had cut into the high, stony bluffs, but they had planned ahead. His horses had been driven off, and without them there just wasn't a chance.

"Walk out," he muttered. He looked skyward. The snow-laden clouds were coming in again, in heavy legions that darkened the skies, shadowed the land, and set the trees to trembling in anticipation.

Walk out . . . he could have made it another time, although the snow was deep and it was fifteen miles to the nearest community, Stokes's store, and the nameless cluster of shacks that had gathered around it.

But not now. Not with the pain gnawing at his belly, not with the deeper pain of betrayal.

"Suck it up, Roland! Move or die." He looked down slope again, shook his head, and started up over the ridge, still holding his stomach, leaving a trail of blood against the new snow.

He was knee-deep in snow much of the way despite his attempts to keep to high ground, to the stony ridges where the wind whipped the snow away. He had packed snow against the fire of his wound, but it hadn't done any good. It was eating him alive with searing pain.

He was halfway to his objective, Stokes's store, before he realized that he had been hit in the shoulder as well. There was a stiffness there that puzzled him until he pulled down the shoulder of his coat and saw the jagged bullet wound. The pain of it was nothing compared to the boring ache in his stomach.

"No chance, my man," Roland said to himself. "You're playing a losing hand."

The storm rolled in and the wind, blustering and howling, slapped at the wounded man, throwing handfuls of snow at his face. It stung like buckshot and

Roland lowered his eyes, bowing his head. The snow was deep, the wind bitterly cold.

He wanted only one thing, warmth. To be warm for one more minute, to feel a fire glowing against his cheek, *not* to feel the terrible cold that chilled the marrow of his bones and made his muscles hard and brittle.

"If I can make it to the store," he muttered. His voice was lost in the shriek and howl of the wind as he trudged down the long mountain slope through the heavy ranks of pines.

It was hours, it was years, eternity, before he spotted the thin, rising finger of smoke against the briefly clearing sky. Before he spotted the dirty cluster of ramshackle buildings low in the valley.

He stood there for a long while, gazing in disbelief at the tiny town. Then he started forward, thinking of one thing, of the iron stove in Stokes's store, of warmth, of a moment's peace. . . .

"Well?" Stokes demanded.

"I can do nothing," Maria said. "It is very bad, a very bad wound."

"Yeah, all right. I can see that. Thanks, Maria. Better pull his shirt down again, okay?"

The stout Mexican woman did so. She glanced at the tall man again and crossed herself.

"Anybody know who this jasper is?" Stokes asked. "I swear I've seen him before, but I can't recollect a name."

"I know him," Handy Cross said. The big man continued to sip at his whiskey. "He had a place up over the hogback."

"Miner, was he?"

"No. No, I don't rightly recall what he was doing. Had him a few horses, I recollect." Handy shrugged.

"Any family up there?"

"No. He was all alone, as I recall."

"He had a brother somewhere," Jake Poole put in. "He was in the army, I believe. Something like that."

"Well." Stokes bent over the wounded man and rested his thumb on the big artery in his throat. Then he lifted an eyelid and shook his head. "Anyone who knows where his next of kin might be had best write. This man's dead."

"He was dead when he walked in the door. Beats me how he lasted."

"Yeah." Stokes sighed. "We'll take him out to the woodshed. When we get a thaw, we'll bury him. What did you say his name was, Handy?"

"Justice. That's the name that'll go on his marker. Roland Justice."

"All right. Let's take him out back. Handy, you can write, can't you? Why don't you start on that letter."

"Where's it going? Hell, no one knows rightly where the man's brother might be. If he does get it, why it'll be too late to do anything about it, won't it? Not much point in writing."

"No, but it's the proper thing to do. Write it. The army will find his brother sooner or later, if he is an army man. At least we'll have done the right thing."

"All right." Handy shrugged. "For all the good it'll do."

He had taken the ink bottle, paper, and pen and seated himself at the far end of the counter to laboriously scratch out the message to the man's next of kin. Handy was right—likely the letter would never reach its intended recipient. If it did, why, it would be months from now, nearly too late even to mourn. Still—you did what was right.

Stokes and Jake Poole carried the body out of the store. They crossed the snow-covered yard and placed the dead man on the floor of the woodshed. Stokes stood looking at the body for a minute and then they went out, leaving Roland Justice to sleep his long sleep.

JOIN THE RUFF JUSTICE READERS' PANEL

Help us bring you more of the books you like by filling out this survey and mailing it in today.

1. Book title:_____

   Book #:_____

2. Using the scale below how would you rate this book on the following features.

Poor		Not so Good			O.K.			Good			Excellent
0	1	2	3		4	5	6		7	8	9	10

	Rating
Overall opinion of book	_____
Plot/Story	_____
Setting/Location	_____
Writing Style	_____
Character Development	_____
Conclusion/Ending	_____
Scene on Front Cover	_____

3. On average about how many western books do you buy for yourself each month?_____

4. How would you classify yourself as a reader of westerns?
   I am a ( ) light ( ) medium ( ) heavy reader.

5. What is your education?
   ( ) High School (or less)   ( ) 4 yrs. college
   ( ) 2 yrs. college   ( ) Post Graduate

6. Age_____   7. Sex: ( ) Male ( ) Female

Please Print Name_____

Address_____

City_____State_____Zip_____

Phone # (_____)_____

Thank you. Please send to New American Library, Research Dept, 1633 Broadway, New York, NY 10019.